Praise

"Unpredictable, touching, and true, *The Life You've Imagined* is a stand-out story; I devoured it and wanted more."

—Therese Anne Fowler, author of
Z: A Novel of Zelda Fitzgerald

"A richly woven story laced with unforgettable characters. Cami, Maeve, Anna, and Amy will snag your heart as they explore the sometimes-wide chasm between hope and reality. A beautiful book."

—Therese Walsh, author of
The Last Will of Moira Leahy

"Backed by Riggle's trademark unflinching honesty and imbued with heart and hope, *The Life You've Imagined* is a terrific novel about love and loss, letting go and holding on. A book to share with family and friends—I loved it."

—Melissa Senate, author of *The Secret Joy*

Praise for *Real Life & Liars*

"This book is a must-read for anyone who has ever been both grateful and driven mad by the people they love most: their family."

—Allison Winn Scotch, author of the
New York Times bestselling *Time of My Life*

"With ease and grace, Riggle walks the fine line between sentimentality and comedy, and she has a sure hand in creating fun, quirky characters."

—*Publishers Weekly*

hope

out

loud

Also by Kristina Riggle

Real Life & Liars
The Life You've Imagined
Things We Didn't Say
Keepsake
The Whole Golden World

hope

out

loud

A HAVEN NOVELLA

KRISTINA RIGGLE

NLA Digital, LLC

This book is a work of fiction. The characters, incidents, and dialogue are drawn from the author's imagination and are not to be construed as real. Any resemblance to actual events or persons, living or dead, is entirely coincidental.

Writers spend years laboring over a single book. Please respect their work by buying their books from legitimate sources. The scanning, uploading, and/or distribution of this book via the Internet or any other means without the permission of the publisher is illegal and punishable by law. Please purchase only authorized electronic editions, and do not participate in or encourage electronic piracy of copyrighted materials. Your support of the author's rights is appreciated.

Hope Out Loud. Copyright © 2015 by Kristina Ringstrom. All rights reserved. Printed in the United States of America. No part of this book may be used or reproduced in any manner whatsoever without written permission except in the case of brief quotations embodied in critical articles and review. Address requests for information to NLA Digital, 1732 Wazee Street, Suite 207, Denver, CO 80202.

Production Manager: Lori Bennett
Cover Designer: Mumtaz Mustafa
Photography: Daniel Sheehan
Book Designer: Angie Hodapp

ISBN 978-1-62051-181-7

Acknowledgments

HEARTFELT THANKS TO MY EARLY READERS, ELIZA GRAHAM and Kelly O'Connor McNees. I'm indebted to you for your talent, insight and courtesy. For guiding me through this new publishing frontier, much gratitude to my agent Kristin Nelson and digital liaison Lori Bennett. For the gorgeous cover, thank you to Mumtaz Mustafa; your work always shines. Many thanks to Angie Hodapp for her beautiful interor design. Thanks to copyeditor Reem Abu-Libdeh for being my safety net and helping me produce proper ellipses. To my brother in law, Bob, thanks for helping me get Anna's career details right. If I screwed any of that up, dear reader, it's my fault, not his. Better yet, assume it's poetic license.

*For Bruce, because sometimes you hope
enough for both of us*

CHAPTER 1

Anna
Monday, July 1, 2013
Chicago

THE HANDWRITING ON THE POSTCARD IS SPIKY AND jerky, as if someone were trying to yank it away from my father before he finished what he had to say. I turn it back to the other side, looking at the cartoonish picture of a pouting little girl in pigtails, her feet turned in, her little round face abject. "Florida's Great, But...I Miss You!"

The postmark, however, says Tennessee.

The Anna of five years ago would have scowled, torn it up, thrown it away, all in a big act to convince myself I couldn't possibly care about the father who had abandoned my mother and me twenty years ago—no, twenty-five years ago, now.

Since he popped back up in 2008, I have consented to let him get in touch by writing. It felt safer, demanding written contact only, as opposed to phone calls or, heaven help me, visits.

The writing bears its own intimacy, though. Emails look uniformly sterile, barring the use of a whimsical font or silly signature line. But something handwritten conjures up the writer. I imagine my dad's knobby fingers clutching his pen as he scrawls away. I wonder what he was thinking when he stuck on the stamp, where exactly in Tennessee he was when he slid it into a mailbox. Does he still limp, like when I saw him last? Has he resorted to a cane by now?

When my cell phone rings, I know without looking that it's my mother. I assigned her a special ringtone: "Bridge Over Troubled Water," one of her very favorite songs. *When you're weary, feeling small...*

"Hi, Mom."

"Hi, honey! I'm so excited to see you! The weather forecast looks great. Is Cami able to come?"

"No, she's so close to popping that kid out that she's fit to burst. She's going to stay near familiar doctors. Not to mention her husband."

When I left Haven, Michigan, five years ago after a turbulent summer, Cami came back to Chicago with me, and we were contented roommates for about a year until she fell head over heels for a flooring contractor she met through her home renovation work. I was secretly relieved to have a place to myself again. Economic necessity forced me to share rent at the time, what with having jumped ship from Partner Track Big

Law to hanging out my own shingle. Once she moved out, though, I grew once again to love the cocooned feeling of a door I can lock against the entire world, best friends and men included. I let people in when I want to, only. I have to admit I want to do that less and less often these days.

My mother sighs theatrically. "Oh. I was hoping she'd risk it, and then end up having the baby here. Naughty of me, I know."

"We'll just have to get you down here to visit, and you can coo to your heart's content." I represent my mother's only shot at grandchildren, and the biological window is open only a hair by now, but she has the good grace not to mention this.

"So Mom, any big plans for the week? I mean, other than Saturday, obviously."

She clears her throat, and I recognize this tell of hers. Oh goody.

"Well, dear, the Beckers invited us to their Fourth of July bash, and I thought we could go."

I was afraid of this.

"Can't we just get a spot on the beach and watch from there? Or heck, do sparklers in the yard and skip the traffic."

"My dear, you are way too young to be that jaded. C'mon, Al wants to go. He's never been to the Beckers'."

"I would have thought your wedding was enough excitement for the week."

"Pshht, excitement, it's just a few people standing on a beach for heaven's sake." I'm still wrapping my brain around the fact that Mailman

Al—the man who would drop off our bills and junk mail at the Nee Nance Store, buy a Diet Coke, and stride off with his postal shorts showing off his knobby knees—is about to be my stepdad.

"Which reminds me, I got another postcard from my father. You?"

We often get notes at the same time. He still thinks of us as one unit, Anna and Maeve, the daughter and wife he left behind to rot in that stupid rundown convenience store which was both our livelihood and our home. My mother might still be there now, ringing up cigarettes and Lotto tickets and Bud Light, if not for being evicted for a classy joint that sells fancy cheese and wine and such.

Mom sighs like I let the air out of her. "Yes."

"Same old?"

"Yes." After a pause, she adds, "Pretty much."

"Uh-oh. What?"

The attorney in me can't help but chase that down. There's a reason she said "pretty much" and a reason she paused first.

"Well, I'd told him about the wedding. He seems a bit, well, taken aback."

I groan and drop my head into my hand. "Mom, why did you tell him? That's just asking for trouble."

"Because I'm not going to hide and pretend and sneak around. I'm not doing a single thing wrong. And he might as well know for sure he hasn't got a reason to come sniffing back around here."

"I hope you didn't tell him the date."

"So what if I did?"

I open my mouth to give her "so what," because he's grossly inappropriate and romantic to a delusional extent and it would be just like him to swoop into town and try to woo her away. Instead I take a breath. I know I'm right, but I've finally learned that sometimes it's better to be quietly right. I smile, so that my voice will come out brighter than I really feel.

"Never mind. I'm sure he's far too busy with his latest scheme anyway, not to mention he probably can't scrape up the gas money to get here from Tennessee."

We hang up after she makes plans to pick me up at the Grand Rapids train station tomorrow. I'll be spending the rest of the week in my hometown, helping her finish up details of her wedding.

In my room I peel off my "lawyer clothes" as I call them. I still wear most of the same suits I did back in my days at Miller Paulson. They're expensive enough to last, and classic enough not to go out of style, and working for myself I don't have the budget for fancy shopping. My suits feel like armor in a not-unwelcome way. By contrast, it makes getting into my pajamas at six thirty a delicious treat.

Shelby, my favorite Miller Paulson friend, always tries to rouse me for happy hour with the old group. They all still love me, she swears, and in fact probably like me better now that I'm outside of office politics.

When I couldn't stand it, the happy hour crowds

and the drinks and the expense and the noise and the chatter about nothing, I begged off with excuses of work, always plausible in our business.

Sometimes she tries to set me up and gets exasperated when I continually turn her down. "You're turning into a hermit! Don't you ever want to get laid again?"

Online dating has served me well and I've not dried up completely; I just saw Kevin last weekend, and we had a nice time with Indian takeout and Netflix. Meanwhile, Shelby's picking out husbands for me. At thirty-six that ship has sailed and I'm happy to wave from the shore. Bon voyage to the suburbs. Enjoy your Popsicle stains.

I do marvel at Cami, though, how quickly her tough façade crumbled to dust as her belly grew, and she'd unconsciously rub it in small, slow circles. That kind of love is like a miracle, a one-in-a-million chance. I wonder if she appreciates this.

I settle into the corner of my sectional with a bowl of Mini-Wheats and the remote control. I found the couch secondhand at a consignment shop. It's not old enough to be cool vintage, and too old to be "gently used," but it's just the right amount of beat-up comfy.

My phone dings at me for a new email, though without even looking I guess who it is, and yep, it's Michelle. Poor thing is going through a funhouse ride of a vicious divorce, and as her attorney, I'm right there beside her. I read it while munching my cereal, then put down my bowl to type back a quick reassurance and hope that will calm her down.

Michelle, I will talk to opposing counsel to attempt to get him to stop, but otherwise, there's very little we can do if he's telling mutual friends you're insane. I'm sure it's not pleasant, but try to remember that we'll get through this. This too shall pass.

Who knew I'd end up ferrying so many people across the raging river of divorce? When I left Miller Paulson, I was thinking mainly of freedom from partner track pressure, office politics, and the emptiness of corporations suing corporations. Then I handled one divorce for an acquaintance, and then a couple more, and now it seems like I spend all day helping people renege on "'til death us do part."

As I channel flip, I spot yet another voyeuristic reality show about shopping for wedding dresses. I watch for the satisfaction of being able to roll my eyes at the histrionics over mermaid style versus ball gown. Like any of that will matter in a few years, when they're throwing dishware at each other, and dragging out their final settlement over who gets the *Fast and Furious* DVD.

In contrast, my low-maintenance mom has designed her own wedding dress. It was the only choice she had left, considering the usual offerings were princessy or slinky styles of the young bride, or the dowdy pastels of the mother-of-the-bride. She won't tell me anything about the dress yet, but I can't wait to see it and I have no doubt she'll look terrific.

Mom has remarked more than once, with exaggerated wistfulness, that it really should be the other way around, when you consider our respective ages and stages. She should be planning my wedding.

Yeah well, my dad shouldn't have left us when I was a little girl.

Hasn't she figured this out by now? We don't get to live the life we've imagined.

CHAPTER 2

Beck
Monday, July 1, 2013
Haven, Michigan

"HI, DADDY," MADDIE SAYS, LOOKING UP FROM HER drawing only for a moment. I let my gaze linger on my daughter as I put down my briefcase and drape my jacket over a kitchen chair.

Golden curls dangle onto her paper, obscuring her handiwork. Crayons lie scattered on the table, each one snatched up and discarded as my budding artist races through the color spectrum, periwinkle to plum to peach, on her latest masterpiece.

Samantha glances up from the pot on the stove. "Hi, Will. Good day?" By the time her sentence is done, her back is to me again.

"It's better now," I answer, ruffling Maddie's

curls. She shrugs her head away from my hand, far too busy to be caressed. "Where's your brother?"

Maddie shrugs. Samantha answers, "He's staring at the fish, what else?"

I head off down the hall to his room decked out in Transformers decals, decorated during one of Sam's campaigns to get Harry to be more like other boys. Harry doesn't mind the decoration. Nor does he give a rip about Transformers, or Star Wars, or Pokémon, or whatever else the boys like these days. All he wants to see, care about, or enjoy are animals in all their forms.

His jet black hair hangs down in his eyes. Sam must have had a busy weekend; normally she keeps him on a rigid bangs-trimming schedule. He's more serene than any other four-year-old I've ever seen, Maddie included, and Maddie at that age could freeze for an entire hour if *Sesame Street* was on.

I touch his shoulder, thinking he might startle, but he barely reacts. "Hi, Dad," he says, his eyes following the lazy ellipses of the fish in his tank. "Did I tell you what I learned today about caterpillars? Mom let me go on the NatGeo site and…"

And he's off. If he doesn't become a zoologist or a vet, we'll have done something seriously wrong. I've never met a person so sure of what he wants.

I fold myself down cross-legged on the floor, watching him watch his fish and letting his happy chatter wash over me.

I used to catch myself imagining that Anna was in the other room, cooking dinner and helping Madeline with her third-grade spelling words. She'd call out, "Honey! Dinner!" instead of Samantha's sharp use of "Will!" that always has the exasperated edge of a substitute teacher.

This was unfair, I know. The Anna of my memory was perfect by virtue of her absence. It would have been nothing like I imagined.

Anyway, the long years eroded those daydreams some time ago. It's only the season. The approaching Fourth of July tends to bring Anna to mind.

"Are you ready, champ?"

Harry nods, not moving from his spot.

A familiar black, bitter swell rises in my chest. I was not supposed to be the weekend dad, make that every-other-weekend and Monday nights. I can't remember why we picked Monday for my weekday "parenting time." I'm sure there was a reason but it seems absurd now. On my weekends with the kids, I drop them off Sunday night and I'm back in twenty-four hours. But it took us so long to achieve our détente, we are both loathe to disrupt it.

Harry finally untangles himself from the floor and wordlessly picks up his bag, his tiny backpack of stuffed animals and animal books that he totes between his two homes. That he does this without protest or argument, because it's all he's ever known, is its own kind of agony.

Maddie, however. Maddie is old enough to remember her family intact.

When I return to the kitchen, Maddie's cherub face, which still has infantlike fullness to the cheeks, has turned a splotchy pink. Her eyes are wet.

"I know you haven't seen Mommy all day because I was at work, but you'll be back tomorrow. I'll take you and Harry out for pizza and a sundae, ok? I promise I'll make it up to you," Samantha says.

Sam never wanted to go back to work, and because of that I pay her generous child support and even alimony. I did this willingly, knowing my part in what happened all too well. But when I questioned why she needed to return to work, why the money I pay her isn't enough, she reminded me coldly that her own mother was single. They lived hand-to-mouth, in constant fear of eviction, utility shut-offs, and doctor bills. In this way Sam reminds me of my Depression-era grandmother who refused to throw away expired food because it was "perfectly good," no matter how wealthy my father became.

Maddie has finally stood up from the chair and is dragging her feet to the little Maddie-height peg on the wall where her own two-household backpack hangs. As much to avoid Sam's glare as anything, I glance down at the artwork she was working on. It was a butterfly, I think. It's hard to tell under the mass of black scribbles now obscuring her masterpiece.

❖ ❖ ❖

Hope Out Loud 13

I flick on the light in my little townhouse duplex. At least it's not a grim apartment in that massive block of buildings where my sister-in-law used to live, full of twentysomethings getting drunk on the weekends and middle-aged divorced men nursing their beers in front of flickering televisions.

It hardly lives up to the Becker manse where I was raised, but for just me, and the kids when I have them, it suits perfectly well. Harry and Maddie pop their backpacks onto their own little pegs on the wall here, a bit of symmetry with their mother's house that I hope they find comforting. Sam has already fed them chicken nuggets and macaroni as is the Monday custody hand-off tradition. It's an easy meal for her, and I don't have to use up my visitation doing a ton of prep and cleanup. I am grateful for this small courtesy. For my part, I always try to return them clean, fed, and rested, not too spoiled. I don't try to one-up her, or buy the kids' affection. I'm not sure she notices, and she definitely doesn't acknowledge, but I finally figured out that asking for credit for not being a dick is, by definition, a dick move.

Paul and Amy will come by in a few minutes, so I set out some cheese and crackers and pull out some glasses, and a pitcher of lemonade I made from powdery mix. I bobble a glass but it bounces harmlessly on my wood-look table. Wedding presents stayed with Sam. This set I bought at Target on clearance.

The kids have zoomed off to their rooms.

One small comfort is that the toys I have here are somewhat of a novelty. They don't have time to get bored of their things like they did when we were all in one household. So if Maddie sulks and drags her feet about coming, at least she has her Barbie house to play with once she arrives, and Harry can feed his hamster.

Paul raps at my door with his rhythmic "shave-and-a-haircut" knock he's used since we were kids, trying to get invited to his big brother's room. I swing open the door and knock twice for "two bits."

"Hey, Will, what's up? I hope you have beer because this day kicked my ass."

Amy steps in behind him, leading Penelope by the hand. I crouch down to her. "Hiya, Pen. Harry's in his room with the hamster. Want to go see?"

Pen has the Becker family's light green eyes, with straight brown hair always combed smoothly with a precise center part. Paul told me once in confidence that this was Amy's real hair color, something she never liked to admit to anyone.

"Say hi to Uncle Will," Amy prompts, but Pen pops a thumb in her mouth in response and scurries off to Harry's room.

Amy shoots me an apologetic smile—as if I'm offended by my sweetly shy niece—and follows after her. Amy has lately seemed more comfortable visiting with the children than sitting with Paul and me.

At the table Paul has a beer open already and is cracking open one for me, too.

"How are you two holding up?" I ask him.

He grimaces a little. "Fine, I guess. We never should have told Pen so early. She only just stopped asking when the baby's coming and why Mommy's tummy isn't big." He flinches at this memory and takes a long pull from the beer. "Aims was just so excited, finally. We got pregnant with Penelope so fast we never thought…well. It will happen. We're going to see a doctor next week, I guess."

"It'll work out. Amy won't rest until it does, if nothing else."

"No kidding."

Paul tips back in his chair and blinks up at the ceiling a few times. "Yeah. Anyway, you know what I heard?"

"Hmmm."

"Anna's coming to the party at Mom and Dad's."

"I doubt it."

"No, seriously, dude. Dad invited Maeve and her boyfriend, and Maeve said that was perfect because she could bring Anna."

"Ah. That means that Anna's mom wants her to come. Not that she will come. Two different things."

"What else is she going to do on the Fourth? Sit in some stupid Holiday Inn room, or in that little shack of a house?"

"Listen to you, big shot. They've fixed up that house."

"You know what I mean. Everyone else in town is going to go, including her mom, so she'll either have to come along or sit and sulk all by herself. And you know Anna's still single."

"Knock it off."

"Whatever. You live like a monk and there's no reason to. It's like you're putting yourself in some kind of divorce jail. It wasn't just your fault."

"Tell that to Sam, her family, and the whole town. I cheated, I'm the bad guy. Case closed."

"Well you can't change that by going on a sex strike for the rest of your days."

Maddie's voice pipes up. "What's a seck stripe?"

I whirl around in my chair. Maddie is behind us, her head cocked to one side, eyes narrowed as if she can decode those words in the air. She's dragging a Barbie by the feet.

"Never mind, Uncle Paul was making a silly joke."

"Tell me the joke. I like jokes."

"It's a grown-up joke. What do you need, kiddo?"

She pulls me out of the room to go fix a Barbie house elevator malfunction as Paul barely suppresses snorting laughter.

I try to put the string-operated elevator back together as Maddie tells me a rambling story of what the Barbies are doing in their house today. My mind drifts to Paul's comment about divorce jail. Yeah, I feel guilty and I damn well should.

I was planning to walk out on my marriage, leave one woman for another, somehow expecting to keep quiet the "slept with my old girlfriend" part from my wife. As it turns out, I have no stomach for lying on that scale and with the slightest prompt I spilled it all to Sam, hanging Anna out to dry in the process, and agreeing, in the end, to try to save our marriage. Of course Anna wanted nothing to do with me after that stunt.

Then Sam and I pulled the classic troubled-marriage blunder and had another baby.

Finally the little plastic piece clicks back into place, pulling the string taut. I pull the Barbie elevator up smoothly. "All better," I tell Maddie. "I fixed it right up."

She rewards me with a smile that shows both of her dimples, and throws her arms around my neck for a hug. Her hair smells like apple-scented shampoo.

CHAPTER 3

Anna
Tuesday, July 2, 2013
Haven, Michigan

THE FLOWERS IN FRONT OF MY MOTHER'S HOUSE spill out a riot of colors. Her garden, in fact, has extended far beyond the little strip of dirt in front of the porch where most of her neighbors have plunked some marigolds or daylilies. She has curved the garden out toward the road, creating raised beds with fountains, elf-sized bridges, and a "gazing ball," which I used to call "idiot globe" when I was a snotty teen, because the shiny balls on concrete pedestals seemed so pointless to my know-it-all self.

God, I was self-righteous. I must have been a terrible bore.

My mom shoves open the door of her creaky Chevy and together we cross the velvety lawn.

This little bungalow isn't in the fanciest part of town, and she clearly puts more time and effort into curb appeal than her neighbors. But she radiates joy when she looks at it, so as far as I'm concerned, she can plant flowers on every square foot if she wants.

The bungalow is a sunny yellow with a moss-green door and shutters. It's hard to believe that this was once Cami's tumbledown childhood home. She has been renting it to my mother these last five years for an amount that's more symbolic than profitable. Cami didn't want to live in it. Too many poignant memories. But she did want it saved, fixed up, looking beautiful the way her late mother would have wanted. It pleases her to know that part of her mother's legacy is still here, being tended to lovingly.

I say aloud, half to myself, "I wonder if Cami will want to move back after the baby? Make some new memories here. Have you guys talked about it?"

Picked up for almost nothing in the real estate meltdown, Mailman Al's home is a pretty, new construction house in Poplar Bluff. He always saved his pennies and never went into debt for much of anything, as opposed to most of the rest of the country. It's a beautiful brick home just minutes from the lake, and there's a pool in the development. It's definitely "big enough for two" as Al had boasted at their engagement barbecue, his blue eyes twinkling, arm around his bride.

My mother drops her purse on a console

table just inside the door. "Well. I don't know. We haven't really."

"Cami is distracted, I'm sure. And you both have fixed it up so beautifully she could find a new tenant in two seconds."

My mother wanders toward the kitchen table and settles down gingerly, as if she's afraid of hurting herself. Her gaze is out the window, where she can see her wild palette of flowers in every hue.

"Mom?"

"I don't know if I can move."

"Oh! Well I'm sure you don't have to. Al can move in here, of course."

Her hand goes automatically to her chest. This still happens, I've noticed, a reflexive reaching for her old wedding ring that used to hang on a chain inside her shirt all those years while she waited for my father to come back and claim her again. Finding nothing there, she instead begins to twist her engagement ring, which is a simple sapphire, and more than she'd wanted at all, having insisted to Al she didn't need a gemstone ring, and that a simple wedding band would do.

"He'd rather not, is the thing. He has rooms all set up there for his kids and grandkids when they visit, and their toys, and well...He doesn't want to disrupt them, he says. The littlest ones only just got used to sleeping in those rooms instead of crying and fussing all night."

I join my mother at the table. "Oh. I suppose I can see that. But you think you can't move in there?"

"It's just…this house." She swallows hard and wipes her face under eyes, leaving tiny brown streaks of makeup. "It's been my only real home."

I swallow down a stab of anger at my father. Instead I cover her hand with mine and squeeze. I'm trying to get used to giving physical affection these days, because I know my mother appreciates it.

"It's not the same as being forced out of the store. This is a happy occasion. Al loves you."

"My flowers."

"Think of the enormous, beautiful garden you can plant there."

My mother pulls her hand back, folds her arms and snorts. "It's a development. They have *rules*. Only so many square feet and crap like that."

"And Al won't move here?"

My mom shakes her head.

"You'll work it out, Mom, I'm sure. What does Al say?"

"He doesn't know it's a big deal. I haven't told him yet."

"Don't you think you'd better? Mom, you're getting married in five days."

"Four if you don't count today. And anyway, just because we get married doesn't mean we have to move right that minute. I haven't even packed a single box and he knows that. He can't be expecting me to close up this house the minute we say 'I do.' Maybe there will be a little…transition time. That's all. Oh! You must be starving! Listen to me, some mother I am, not even feeding you after that long train ride. I made some egg salad just the way you like it and I've sliced up fresh vegetables."

And she's off, bustling around the small, sunny kitchen, the only hint of our talk being a slight brown smudge under her eyes.

I can hardly believe my mother is fixing to get married and remain living separate from her husband—just as she did, rather against her will, for twenty years hitched to my absent father.

Aunt Agatha's boutique has become one of my favorite places in all of Haven. It's unapologetically old-fashioned, just as Agatha herself. Doilies drape everywhere, quaint instrumental music wafts out of tinny speakers, and rose-scented potpourri tickles the nose. Faceless white mannequins pose with wedding gowns and prom fashions, leaning backward at the hips as no real person ever does in life.

So much has changed, and this place has not, and for that I'm ever more grateful with each passing year.

I do a double-take to see Mailman Al—I really should stop thinking of him that way—follow us into the store. "Maeve! It's been too long. Almost a whole hour since I've seen your face."

He plants a smooch right on my mom's cheek and for this I have to look away. It might be cute, but it's also my mom and it's all the more nauseating. It also makes me feel nervous to see Al so demonstrative. It's a spooky echo of my dad at his best: over the top, affectionate, and jocular. It was for this version of Robert Geneva that my mother held out all those years, wearing her wedding ring under her shirt.

I hadn't known Al had it in him, until lately. He was just the guy with the mail and a pleasant smile. Retirement and engagement have done wonders for him, I guess. Or he was always this way and I'd never noticed. You get to know people in their roles and you begin to imagine that's all there is to see.

Agatha strolls out of the back room and I swallow back a gasp. She's aged so much in the last five years. She intended to retire back then, but instead hired my mother to help her with the alterations her own arthritic hands could no longer manage. Today, of course, my mother is not here as an employee. Today she is a customer. A bride.

"Maeve! Lovely to see you. Al, it's rotten luck for you to be here, you know."

"Oh, I won't stay for the big reveal. But we're having lunch at Doreen's and I couldn't resist popping in to see my girl. Luck though, pssht. I didn't see my first wife in her wedding dress either and she went and died of cancer before we got to retire, so don't talk to me about superstition."

Al's comment has thrown a black cloak over the room, but jovial still, he doesn't notice. His wife passed so long ago, maybe he's woven her loss into the fabric of his life and the fact of her death fails to jar him. Or maybe he's faking it.

With enough practice, a person can seem stoic about damn near anything.

My mother has gone quiet and still. She looks thoughtful, her gaze somewhere on the carpet in front of her shoes. Al kisses her goodbye, announces he'll be waiting for her at Doreen's, and he whistles his way out of the room. It takes me a moment to place the tune. *Going to the chapel and we're gonna get married...*

"Well," Agatha says, clapping her hands once. "Shall we?"

My mom swallows hard and follows her to a dressing room. I perch on one of the little couches around a raised platform near the center of the store. About the only thing I can look at is my own reflection in the giant three-paneled mirror across from me. I look so much like my mother. My penny-colored hair doesn't have threads of gray yet. My skin is somewhat smoother—no longer dewy with youth, either—but the curls, the freckles; even my posture echoes Maeve Geneva.

I'm not often susceptible to bridal daydreaming, but sitting here surrounded by the gowns, the jewelry, the display of pointy white shoes...even I succumb to a wistful sigh. If only...if only what? If only my marriage examples hadn't been such rubbish. My parents' marriage was a farce. My best friend Cami's father turned into a raging abusive drunk when his wife died young. And how many young marrieds at the law firm crumbled under the weight of partner-track workload? And now I spend two-thirds of my working life helping people split up.

If only Beck—no. That train of thought leads nowhere good.

My mother is right. It is odd to be the daughter, sitting on the couch, waiting for my fifty-something mom to come out in her dress. It stirs up odd thoughts, too. I suck in a deep breath and huff it out, trying to bring myself back to the present happy occasion.

And here she comes.

"Oh, Mom. Oh, it's stunning. Just beautiful."

It's a cream-colored sheath style dress. The V-neck bodice features a top layer of diaphanous fabric that knots at the center of her bosom, and then wraps around her waist where it falls to the ground, with a tiny bit of train. The skirt is a creamy silk that skims the top of her feet with a slit just to the knee. It's the perfect blend of romantic and attractive, of dignified yet pretty and bridal.

Agatha leads my mother to the raised platform. Mom keeps her shining eyes on me, instead of turning around to see herself. Agatha flutters around her, fluffing out the train, picking off invisible pieces of lint.

"Your mother designed this," Agatha declares with all the pride of a mother herself. "I did the fitting and machine sewing, but the fine work she did herself. If I thought she'd ever leave Haven I'd sign her up for *Project Runway*."

My mom chuckles, still not turning around.

Hope Out Loud

Finally Agatha takes her shoulders and steers her to face herself. She gasps, and puts a hand to her chest. Agatha turns to me. "We're going to pin just a flower in her hair. Maggie at Haven Floral already tested it out and it's going to look great. This dress doesn't need a lot of fuss, does it?"

I'm not listening carefully though, because Mom looks pale. Her freckles stand out bright, like spangles against her pinkish skin. I rise to stand by her, worried about her blood pressure. Back in the waning months of the store, she'd once collapsed right in the aisle from a blood pressure spike.

Finally Mom seems to remember that we're here, we are waiting for a reaction. "It is lovely, isn't it? Feels wrong somehow to praise my own work. The sin of pride, my mother would say."

Agatha snaps, "She's dead, so who cares. Sorry, love, that was harsh."

Mom laughs, sounding a little relieved. "No, you're too right. Who cares, indeed? Well. Let's get out of this thing before I break into a sweat and ruin it."

Once we make it to the sidewalk, I stop Mom from zooming off to lunch by placing a hand on her arm. "Mom? Are you all right? What was wrong back there?"

"Wrong? Nothing at all." Her laugh is high-pitched and strange.

"Mom."

"I guess I'm a lousy liar." She squints past me in the July sun. "It's just...the first thing I saw when I looked in that mirror was your father next to me. I know, it's ludicrous and I don't want him back, I promise. But when we first met, got engaged, I imagined being his bride and it never got to happen. We had to run off and elope because my mother was so angry, and we didn't have any money ourselves for a wedding. I just wore a sundress and we were on the courthouse steps and for years I tried to convince myself it was romantic that way. Instead it turned out to set the tone for the whole marriage. Everything we ever had was makeshift, jury-rigged, and temporary plans that turned permanent."

She looks at me fully, and reaches up to touch my face, startling me again with how much taller I turned out to be. I forget this all the time, living so far away. "Except you, darling. You were the one perfect thing we made together and for that alone, I have no regrets at all."

Mom tried to include me for lunch, but I can't get used to this particular triad yet of me, my mother, and her boyfriend, now fiancé. I waved her off instead, but as soon as I did, I found myself at loose ends.

So I settled on the sunny side of a street bench next to a tree, enjoying the balmy warmth. The old Nee Nance Store is just a couple of blocks away. I could go visit the new place, maybe even ask to go upstairs and see my old room. It was a little nook with a gabled roof and its own octagon-shaped window. It's probably gutted, though.

Torn up and rehabbed into offices, or maybe a swank studio apartment suitable for living above a shop that sells fancy olive oil. That was rather the point of evicting us, after all.

My phone chimes as a text comes in. I shade the screen and squint at it. It's Poor Divorcing Michelle. In a moment of sentiment before I left, when I fielded her call during a quick stop to the office, I'd given in to her sniffling request to share my cell phone number, in case of emergencies. Of course, when your entire life is being ripped in half by a bitter divorce, when your kids hang in the balance, every single thing is an emergency. Anyway, her husband has been such a bullying asshole, she needs all the help she can get.

"Oh shit," I say aloud, causing an older tourist with silvery hair to huff in my direction as she passes. I pull a face at her retreating back before I tell Michelle that I'll get a hold of her husband's lawyer and make him comply with the temporary custody order. It's her turn with the kids, and he won't bring them over. It's a classic tune in the divorce repertoire.

The husband's attorney is a decent enough sort of guy and when I call with my Stern, Indignant Lawyer Voice (patent pending) I'm sure he'll make his client get with the program. It could be worse. The bullying husband could be my client.

I heave myself up from the bench and go back to my mom's car, so I can perform this rant in private.

Opposing counsel doesn't pick up, so I scold

his voicemail and demand a call back. I follow that up with an email to the same effect, typed as fast as I can manage with my thumbs. Then I have to jump out of the car before I roast alive with the July sun steaming up the parked Chevy. I walk toward the beach in search of a breeze, all the better to re-enter the pleasant vacation zone.

The streets are crowded with tourists and locals, and it's easy to sort them out. The tourists are richer, for one thing. They've got natty clothes with branded logos. Not that we don't have our share of money in Haven but it's concentrated in a few enclaves and private spaces. Those folks tend to remain there, barbecuing on their spacious decks overlooking the lake or the golf course. The locals out and about now are the ones in jean shorts or khaki capris, grabbing a sandwich before heading back to sell lighthouse tchotchkes or sit at the lifeguard stand, or maybe answer phones at the accountant firm upstairs from the shoestore.

The sun winks off the lake in the distance, and the sounds of laughing children and waves undulating over the sand saturates the atmosphere such that we seem to forget all this beauty and joy. But those merry tourists swinging their shopping bags can't help but gaze at their surroundings.

And then I spot it, feeling ambushed, as if my old home had jumped out to get me. As I stop short to gawk at the shiny, aggressive modernity of the place, a mother rams into me with her stroller. So I step out of the flow, where I rest one hip against a newspaper box.

The front windows used to hold faded beer ad posters, and the lettering read NEE NANCE STORE, named after my own babytalk attempt to say convenience store, back when my parents were still young marrieds getting a start.

Now gold sans serif lettering on sparkling clean glass reads VIN FROMAGE. I hold my hand over my face to hide my smirk. Not wine *and* cheese, but wine cheese? This reminds me of a running joke I had with Beck, way back when. We went out to Portobello for dinner before a Valentine's dance, and the waiter conspicuously and sniffily corrected Beck's pronunciation of "bruschetta." For the rest of that meal and ever after we would intentionally mispronounce any fancy or foreign food name. We called crème brulee "Creamy Broolee" and jalapeños "jalopy-noes." To this day I mispronounce menu items in my head and smile. If we were still in touch, I'd call him and laugh about Vin *Fro*-Midge.

Well, now I've got to go in.

It had been some unspoken pact that my mother and I avoid the place. My heart hurts on her behalf when I think of all the time she wasted in that crumbling liquor store. I'm the lucky one. I got out.

As I step through the door, I have to admit it really is lovely inside. It smells delicious, for one thing, savory and spicy. A small deli section sells fresh sandwiches back where our Hi-C

Fruit Punch used to be. The clerk gives me the tight smile of the busy service worker who acknowledges your presence but doesn't have time to gab. He looks to be a college kid. I wander past where we used to have the beer cooler—now home to a whole wall of wine—and look for the door to the upstairs. I can't find it.

Should I ask to see upstairs? Small-town people will allow quite a lot, especially if you can identify yourself as a native.

Being in this building gives me a pang for my daffy aunt Sally. My dad may have bailed on me, but his sister stuck around, keeping us laughing with her antics and her crazy wigs. I'd walk into the Nee Nance and she'd laugh about a "Geneva Convention" every single time. I used to roll my eyes, but now that she's gone, what I wouldn't give to hear that stupid old joke again.

"Don't tell me you're moving back."

I whirl around to see Beck standing there with a crooked smile and one sandy curl loose on his forehead. My heart races double-time and my mouth goes dry. We'd broken up—the final time, that is—almost in this very spot. Five years ago, he came to the store to beg me to give him time to sort things out. Time he would spend going home to his wife. I'd seen him briefly at Sally's funeral, but otherwise had managed to avoid Beck sightings, getting news of his life only from third parties, and only when such news was foisted upon me. I'd deleted his contact and texts from my phone, thrown away the copy of *Walden* he gave me, and carried on with my life hundreds of miles away.

My instinct is to blurt, *What are you doing here?* But his office is just down the way; he's probably here three times a week. My hand goes up to fuss with my own hair, a fidget that took me years to break, but still rears its ugly head when I'm surprised. My shocked brain finally catches up to real time and I realize he asked me a question.

"Had to finally look around. Can't help but think of old times."

I look down, away from his eyes, the color of pale green sea glass. This comment, between any other two people, would be meaningless. But the last time we saw each other, we'd been having an affair that nearly destroyed his marriage. Maybe it did, in fact, destroy the marriage. Their divorce happened years later, but I'm sure our cheating opened up a generous fault line. Old times indeed.

"I know what you mean," he says. "It's so funny seeing you here, in your old place, but it's not your place."

"Come here often?" I rejoin, rolling my eyes at my own lame joke. I glance around the store, looking for anyone here who would know us, know our history. This scene would make rich fodder for the magpies down at Doreen's.

"Not so often. But Dad wanted me to grab some wine for dinner tonight. Amy and Paul are coming by, you should join us."

I laugh bitterly before I can stop myself.

It was Paul, Beck's brother, who redeveloped the Nee Nance and kicked my mother out. All's well that ends well, et cetera. Nevertheless, I don't relish sharing a dinner table with Paul Becker.

"I'll pass, thanks." I swallow hard, so thirsty that I would like to snatch a Coke right out of the cooler and glug it down, corn syrup, calories, and all. I feel just as overheated now as I did in my mom's car minutes ago, though I can hear the air conditioning roaring away in here.

Beck doesn't back away, or move to leave. He tilts his head to catch my eye again. "How are you doing? Has your dad been...is he in touch?"

"Sometimes. I get postcards."

"Is that okay for you?"

In the five years since I moved away, again, I'd forgotten this. I'd forgotten what it's like to be in the presence of a man who knows every scuff mark and scratch and stain in the house that is your personal history. Beck also knows how it makes me feel. He knows enough to ask. My shoulders relax a degree or two. I hadn't realized I was tense.

"Yes. Most of the time it is." My old self would not like to admit this, not even to him. And now that I've gone this far, I wish I could blurt it all out to him. Often, I wish my dad stayed away, and in fact sometimes I even wish he would die—quick and painless of course. Then I could mourn him properly and move on. This quasi-contact—sort-of-there, sort-of-not—messes with my head in a whole different way than his stark absence. How can he settle for only postcards? Doesn't he want to know what he missed? Is it because I didn't give him grandchildren? Would he have cared in that case? I look up at Beck again. "Did I ever tell you he has another family?"

"What? You're kidding."

"No. A common-law wife. Or at least he did, last I knew. There are twin boys. They'd be almost twenty by now, I think."

"Half-brothers."

I shrug. I never wanted to see the children my dad decided to raise instead of me. He offered to send pictures once, and I told him not to.

A woman's voice trills from the doorway of the shop. "Will Becker! Great to see you!"

Beck pastes on a smile before turning around. He and Paul, as the heirs to Becker Development dynasty, walk around in a kind of small-town spotlight.

"Hi there! Fancy running into you here. I hope we can go over the ad copy later? I'm free for lunch in fact." She turns her smile to me, and her expression takes on the blank fakeness of the networking Chamber of Commerce type. This is the face of someone who hasn't decided yet if I'm worth her time. "Hello, I'm Amanda Schafer."

"I'm Anna Geneva."

I see my name register in the way she blinks rapidly and says, too brightly, "Oh! Yes! I think your family used to own this place, right?"

"Sort of. We owned a business that leased

here. I'm in town and thought I'd pop by and check it out. It's nice."

Beck runs his fingers through his hair and clears his throat. "Amanda works for the agency that's taking over the marketing and ads for Becker Dev."

Amanda mock-slaps Beck's arm. "Works for it! Try that I own it, thank you very much. Anyway, lunch, Will?"

"I already ate, Mandy. Just stopped in here on an errand and I have to get back. I'll check my calendar when I get back to the office."

Amanda tosses her sleek dark hair, bobbed to razor precision at her chin. "Well then, I'll leave you to your errand, and your...catching up. Bye!" She pivots on a very high heel and strides out without having bought anything.

I watch Beck watch her leave, his gaze skimming over her body. She's very pretty, svelte and young. This is exactly why I so rarely visit Haven. All this place does is remind me of what's gone for good.

"I'm going to head out," I tell Beck, making to step past him toward the door. He puts one hand on my elbow, barely touching me, but it's enough to send a chill racing up my arm.

"Will you come to my family's Fourth of July? I'd love to see you."

"I don't know. It's a bit more déjà vu than I have the stomach for."

"We'll just have to stay out of the upstairs bedrooms this time."

"God, Beck."

"Sorry. Crummy joke. But, seriously. Please come. You have to save me from Mandy."

"You didn't look like you wanted saving just now."

A blush tinges the tops of his ears. "Fine, she's nice to look at. Listening to her talk for more than ten minutes is a whole other experience. And I think I've still got nail marks on my inner arm from the last time we were at an event and she clung to me the whole time."

"You're sweeping me off my feet."

He takes a step closer to me, and cups his hand around my arm, gently, just above the elbow. He strokes my arm with his thumb. He used to do this all the time, I doubt he even realizes he's doing it now. His face has softened, shedding the last of the awkward tension of our random meeting. He's once again the Beck I always knew, sweet and kind. Too kind for me, I always believed.

"Please come? I just want to catch up a little, before you disappear again to the big city."

I ponder the alternative, which is sitting around alone while everyone else in Haven is making merry somewhere, either at the beach or at a house party. I've done that enough in Chicago. Standing here in front of someone who has known me and cared about me for more years than I want to count, it seems ludicrous to say no.

"Yes, fine. I'll come."

The way Beck lights up at this takes ten years off of him, and I can't help but smile back. As I watch him buy his wine and head out into the sunshine, still wearing that smile, I find myself envying his happy naiveté, in which catching up with an old lover is nothing but a pleasant way to spend an evening, with no corroded emotional freight banging along behind him.

CHAPTER 4

Beck
Thursday, July 4, 2013

MY EYES SNAP OPEN AT SIX THIRTY ON THE DOT.

I can sleep in today, and God I wish I would. There should be some benefit to having to give up my kids on these holidays. I should at least catch some extra sleep.

Years of rigorous punctuality at Becker Dev have conditioned me to dawn wakefulness, not to mention years of being bounced awake by early-bird children. Mornings are still the worst. Those and the holidays I can't have them. Actually, even the holidays they spend with me are awful, because I know they miss their mother.

I turn over in my bed and shove my face under my pillow. I have hours and hours before I can go anywhere or do anything useful. The office is closed today, and the party won't start until seven. Sam's taken the kids to Indiana by now to see her folks. I'll be lucky to get a phone call. I used to try to get the kids to do a video chat with Sam's smartphone, but Harry never seemed to know how to talk to me in that tiny little screen, and Maddie was too busy to look at me. Samantha would end up standing there holding the phone by my daughter's face as she dressed a Barbie or colored a picture, and I'd hear my ex-wife muttering with increasing impatience, "Take the phone and talk to your father."

I tried to be goofy with it, even showing them my nose hairs and making my eyeball huge in the phone. But kids of divorce are smart enough to know that all the wacky hijinks in the world can't cover up the reason for my absence.

Maddie doesn't remember that she almost drowned five years ago, thank god. And even if she remembered she likely couldn't understand that almost losing her—right under my nose, even—makes her rejection sting all the more. She's only a little girl, I continually remind myself. I can't guilt trip her into loving me more.

No more than Sam could do that to me, try as she might.

I sit up on the edge of the bed, tossing my pillow across the room and giving up on sleep. Even though Anna said she'd come and I'm glad I get to see her, I do wish I had the power to skip today entirely.

❖ ❖ ❖

After I make myself a big breakfast and clean the kitchen rigorously to eat up some time, I take myself for a morning stroll around the neighborhood. I'm on my second mile when my phone rings. I happen to be in front of the playground and I stop to take the call, then start walking again. Lone men with no kids around look weird at playgrounds. Besides, I can't handle the sight of gleeful children today.

"Hello?"

"Hello, dear. Did I catch you at a bad time?"

"No, Mom. It's fine. Just taking a walk. What's up?"

"Did I hear correctly that Anna Geneva is coming?"

"Sure. You invited her mother and fiancé, and Anna is in town for their wedding."

"Oh, that's right. Well. Be careful around your father. Maybe don't mention her in front of him." She has dropped her voice and I can tell from the echoing that she's in the mudroom off the garage.

"He can't still be holding that grudge."

"He has a long memory, you know that."

"But he loved Anna when we were kids."

"I think that's why he was so upset by what happened. He trusted her."

"It's not only her fault."

"Nor is it only yours," my mother observes. I can hear her dry tone and just imagine one eyebrow raised. "It takes two to tango."

"Yes, and we tangoed five years ago, and for that matter we only *tangoed* once." I don't remind my mother about the emails, texts, and occasional visits we had in the meantime. She knows it all anyway.

"I'm on your side, Will, you don't have to tell me. And I keep trying to tell your father that things were rocky with you and Samantha anyway. But he likes simple explanations, you know that."

"If he's that upset, why did he invite her mother?"

"That was Paul's doing. He still feels guilty about the store. And anyway, her mother is lovely, we always thought so when we were practically in-laws, back when you kids were dating in school. Will, are you busy today? You should come early. Spend some time with us before the hordes descend."

"Let's see, I have to avoid mentioning Anna Geneva to my father, because he's been angry for five years, gee, I can't wait."

"Please, Will. It's crazy how seldom we see you considering we're right in this same tiny town, and you and your father working together! When was the last time you saw him when you both weren't wearing business suits?"

Knowing the alternative is to watch the shadows creep across the floor in my duplex as a baseball game drones on the television, I admit defeat and agree that yes, I'll come early. The dutiful oldest child will come pay his respects.

✤ ✤ ✤

What I see, as I drive up the huge semicircle driveway in front of my massive childhood home, is a monument to my father's disappointment in me.

I was supposed to want a house for myself at least this big, and fill it with a pretty wife and as many children as she would agree to have. Nannies and maids, too. I lacked the bloodlust for the family business and got sidetracked into a degree in environmental science. So yes, I work for the family shop but seeing as I spend my days picking over site plans for proper drainage and voicing concern over runoff pollution, I'm a thorn in their side more than anything else. Supposedly my intervention in-house keeps them from running afoul of environmental laws. That's the story, anyhow.

Also, having an "environmental projects specialist" is a fun thing to slip into an Earth Day press release.

My brother Paul did get the development bug, but he had the misfortune of coming of age during the housing collapse. Rumor around town was that my father almost lost our family home by taking out mortgages to keep the company afloat during this time. I wouldn't know if that's true. If it ever was, he pulled his ass out of the fire just in time, because the sprawling mansion with its Greek-like columns is still here, looking as embarrassingly grand as it ever did in my childhood.

I pull my Prius into the wide driveway in front of the garage and take a fortifying breath. Everywhere I turn is the ghost of what I used to be.

My sister-in-law's goofy Labrador, Frodo, comes charging around the corner to greet me, his tongue flapping drool behind him. I look for Amy, or Penelope, but instead it's my mother who follows along behind. "Will!" she cries, opening her arms and breaking into a trot, as if I'm coming home from a journey around the globe. I scratch Frodo's ears and then my mother squeezes me around my middle. I leave one arm around her shoulder as we stride across the lawn.

"I see their dog, so Amy and Paul must be here."

"They're inside with Penelope. Frodo was running like a wild thing through the house so I took him out to throw a ball around. You know it's fun having a granddog? I can wind him up and spoil him and give him back when he's difficult. Just like with the grandkids!"

When I don't reply, my mother squeezes me around the waist in a sideways hug. We walk the rest of the way to the house in silence, both of us missing my children.

The sun has swung closer to the earth, sending all our shadows reaching long across the grass. People come by to say hello, talk some business, but then they wander off abruptly as they catch me looking over their shoulders at the driveway, or when I lose the thread of their small talk.

I should have stayed home. The emptiness knifes through me, so much so I even miss Sam.

I switch my beer to my left hand and rub the condensation off my right on the leg of my khaki shorts. My dad takes me by surprise by coming up on my left.

"Looking for someone?" he asks, with a nod toward the stream of arrivals striding up the sloping lawn.

"Not really." I make a point of gazing at the distant twinkling lake.

He sighs, a classic world-weary William Becker Sr. sigh. "You know, son, I'd think you would want a fresh start."

"I'm not looking for a start of any kind, Dad."

"You're young yet. Not even forty. You could still find a nice girl and make it work. But not if you keep going backward. High school is over, Will. Move on."

"Who says I haven't?"

My dad doesn't answer because he's spotted someone over my shoulder. He brightens and waves. When I turn around I see Mandy prancing her way over with a huge red-lipped smile.

"Amanda!" my dad roars in his networking voice.

Lower, he says to me, "She's a nice girl. Don't treat her like she has leprosy."

I remind myself that it's not Mandy's fault that my dad pushes us together, micromanaging my life even now. So I greet Mandy with a friendly smile and accept a cheek kiss, but at the same time I hear a loud, rattly engine pull up and a creaky car door open. There's only one party guest I can think of who drives a car like that. Maeve and Anna have arrived.

CHAPTER 5

Anna
Thursday, July 4, 2013

AL KEPT UP A STREAM OF COMMENTARY ABOUT TIGERS baseball all the way here. I'd ended up in the backseat rather than split up the lovebirds in the front, and my mother drove.

She made little listening noises, but I could tell from the tense set of her shoulders she wasn't hearing a thing.

We'd had one more talk about her reluctance to move into Al's house, but she hadn't found the courage to say a word to her fiancé yet. Nor had she packed a single box. I'd figured out enough to know that Al was a pretty easygoing guy, but I'm sure he expects his wife to actually live with him.

My mother even said, yesterday when we were pulling weeds in the garden, she didn't know if she should actually marry him. She'd rocked back on her heels, pushed up her wide-brimmed hat and said, "Maybe the house is only an excuse. Maybe I don't really want to marry him at all so I'm letting this house thing become a big deal."

I tried to tell her that was nonsense, she was just worried about transition, they loved each other, but my words ran off her like drops of rain. I felt their falseness, too. What did I know about it, anyway? Closest I came to marriage was Marc, and the minute he pushed me about having kids I dumped him.

My mother won't talk about it tonight, I can tell. He's too happy, and she cares too much to ruin that. Ironic, really.

It takes my mom an extra moment or two to get out of the car, as if she's bracing herself for something. Al barely notices, popping out of the passenger side and rocking the car with a firm door slam. He even slams doors happily.

By the time she turns to face her intended, she's got a beaming, sunny smile. She adjusts her floppy pink hat to keep the streaming late-day rays from burning her fair Irish skin, and takes Al's hand.

I plod along behind, feeling not a little like a child again, ever the third wheel.

As Mom and Al look for a cocktail, the first party guests I see are Beck and his father, and…oh yes. Amanda the ad agency woman. That is, Mandy.

I approach to say hello. I almost can't help

it, in fact. They are too close to the driveway. Walking past without acknowledging them would be rude. Amanda laughs at something William Sr. has said, and in doing so takes a half-step closer to Beck, almost as if her merriment has caused her to stumble into him. Her hand slips around him, lightly, as if she doesn't want him to notice.

Amanda's face lights up with her impeccable false smile. "Anna! That's right, isn't it? Anna? How nice to see you."

It sounds proprietary, how's she's greeting me, standing next to the host and the son.

Beck steps away from both of them and reaches around my shoulders for an embrace. He buries his face in my frizzy curls and whispers, "Thank God."

When Beck steps back, he takes my hand. "I'm going to get this girl a drink."

I rarely allow myself to be led around by the hand, but I'm so surprised that I go along for the ride.

He murmurs, "Are they watching? Glance back casually."

I sneak a look back while I pretend to fuss with a barrette. "Yes. Your dad has his arms folded. Amanda is standing so close she looks like she might try to eat him."

"She might at that." He adds, after a quick glance at my legs, "You look pretty today."

He always was a leg man, Beck. I'm glad I bothered to shave.

In the tent, Beck orders me a pinot grigio and I wink at him. "You mean 'peanut Gregory'?"

It takes him a few beats to remember our old joke. "Right, of course. Only the finest in peanut gregory at Chez Becker," he replies, pronouncing the *chez* with a hard "ch" and a distinct "z."

He accepts a Stella Artois and immediately starts peeling the label. He walks away from the throng, toward the bluff over the lake, so I follow. "So how many dates have you two had?"

"Who?"

"I'm not talking about Eleanor Roosevelt, Beck."

"Two or three. How did you know?"

"She had at least some basis for being possessive of you. Most women won't jump to that without at least a little encouragement. I assume these were recent dates?"

"Fairly. Is this a cross-examination?"

"Direct, I'd say. Anyway, relax. I'm just curious."

"My dad would do cartwheels if we got together. He's got this imaginary checklist, as if that's all you need. Ambitious, nice, attractive, she fits in." He mimes ticking boxes on a page.

Fits in. Exactly as I never did, the frizzy-haired freckled girl who lived over a liquor store. Oh, the Beckers were gracious as could be and fawned over my grades and accomplishments. But they never expected our love to be permanent; high school love never is. It was easy enough to let our romance run its course.

"Your dad didn't seem very warm to me tonight."

"Well. He's not very warm to me either lately."

He doesn't have to elaborate. I get it. I'm sure people are still talking about it now, watching us silhouetted on the bluff in the pink of the setting sun.

That's Anna Geneva. She had an affair with him five years ago. Oh, he tried to save the marriage...

I look up at Beck. He's gazing out over the lake. A breeze is ruffling his hair. He's squinting into the sun, a frown marring his face that used to be so happy, optimistic. He was so ready to go against the grain to become a tree-hugger in a family of land-devouring builders. Then again, it's easy to be brave at seventeen.

I ask him, "Do you ever want to just leave? Get out and start over where nobody knows you? It's refreshing, actually. A big old reset button. I ought to know, I've done it twice."

"Liquor store to law firm to private practice."

"Something like that, yeah."

He turns to me. "But are you happy? Out there by yourself?"

I open my mouth with a reflexive yes, but the expression on his face stops me. He expects honesty, and he deserves it.

"Well. I'm not sad. And sometimes 'not sad' has to be enough."

He looks back out over the lake, sets his beer down in the grass, and jams his hands in his pockets. "It's academic anyway. I can't move away from the kids."

Of course he can't, just like I can't stay away

from my mother's home in Haven, no matter how far away I live.

For long moments we both face the lake, watching the reddening sun sink into the haze. The waves from up here sound distant, a whispered "shh" on the cusp of sleep.

Beck reaches around my shoulders and draws me in. We stand side by side, fitting together like we did twenty-five years ago, when anything at all seemed possible.

"We should get back to the party," Beck says, stretched out on the grass by now, his legs in front of him, his shoes abandoned next to him. He's propped up on his hands. My posture is the same, except my legs are demurely crossed, seeing as I'm wearing a knee-length sundress.

"You know what? I'm too damn old for 'should'. Why? We don't want to mingle, so let's not. I spent so much of my life racing toward 'should' and all it earned me was a fancy condo I was too busy to ever be in, and eventually didn't even want. You know what they think of us already. They'll think the same whether we fake-smile our way through the party or not."

"My dad won't be happy."

"And you're not a child." I cringe at my tone. "Sorry, that came out sharper than I intended."

"No, you're right. I feel like I'm frozen in time here in this town. I can't leave."

"The kids. I know."

"Not just them. My whole career of sorts

has been with my dad's company. If I were to leave, what would I do? Where would I go? Any employer would look at the nepotism and think, 'Yeah, this guy has had a sweet ride his whole life and wouldn't know hard work if it bit him'. Not true. I mean, I do work hard. But yeah. I've also had it easy."

I scoot closer. "Maybe materially, but that's not the only thing that counts. And if you emphasize the projects you've done, instead of the name of the company, you could still make an impression. Hell, consult and hire yourself out."

He turns to me and smiles sadly. "You always did know just what to do. And you were brave enough to just go out and do it."

"It wasn't bravery. Bravado, mostly. Not the same thing."

We both turn toward a loud pop. Someone down the beach is setting off firecrackers. The sky is deepening from pale gray-blue of dusk to a velvety dark, yet it's not quite there. It's that in-between time: later than dusk, not quite night.

A voice from the party, maybe Paul, bellows that it's time to go down to the water and arrange the chairs and blankets. There's a private sliver of beach down a set of wooden switchback stairs. Beck looks at me. "We're not going down there, are we?"

"We're sure not. Especially considering five years ago."

I wish I hadn't said it out loud. Now we're both thinking of it. Back then, I'd gone down the stairs trying to evade people, forgetting that they'd be gathering for the fireworks. I'd been standing apart from the crowd with my feet in the waves, lost in thought, when I'd spotted Madeline's gold hair floating in the water and dove in after her. The memory still makes me seize with fear, even knowing that she's fine. Then there's all that came after.

Beck only says, "It's over now. All of it is over."

I spread my cardigan down behind me in the grass and lie straight back, so I can watch the stars wink to life overhead. I sense Beck stretch out, too, and I allow myself some nostalgic pleasure at his closeness. I'm not even surprised when I feel his fingers entwine with mine. Nor do I pull my hand away.

The first starburst of color explodes over our heads. Beck must be thinking the same thing I am. We spent a few July fourths just this way, stretched out in the grass, side by side, well away from everyone else. It was the closest thing to privacy two teen-agers in a small town could ever get, outside of a car's backseat.

His fingers pull away. A rustle of grass. I turn my head to face him. He has sat up on his side now, propping his head on his hand. He's staring at me, and I stare back, though we can't see much now that the sun has truly gone and the only lights are yards away at the house, or pinpricks of color in the sky far above. He could be sixteen again. Me too.

"Anna."

I can't tell if this is a question or a beginning.
"Beck."
"Can I kiss you?"
"Yes," is my unconsidered answer.

And so he does, his face blotting out the fireworks, the sky, the last twenty-five years of screw-ups and confusion. Kissing him here, like this, is coming home.

We did it all backwards. Our teenage love was uncomplicated and easy. We had a friendship of like minds plus passionate ardor; hesitant virgins making clumsy love in a moonlit park. Our drama and crises came later, when we should have been old enough to know better. As it turned out, we were merely old enough to take something lovely and ruin it.

He's nearly on top of me now, and the pressure of him is reassuring and safe. So is the feeling of his hand in my hair, on my shoulder, my breast through my clothes. I smile under his kiss and he stops long enough to ask, "What?" with a teasing edge in his voice.

I smile, then pull him down to me by the back of his neck. I won't try to explain how delightful and sweet this is, our slow fumbling, fully dressed, just like kids. I can't remember the last time I felt so innocent.

He pulls back and whispers in my ear, his voice husky, "The house is empty. C'mon, let's go in."

The illusion falls away like windblown ash. The house was empty five years ago, too, when we screwed in the guest room and he was still married, his little girl white-faced in the hospital.

I sit up so quick I almost bash his face, and then I scramble backwards on the grass.

"No."

"Anna..."

"Look at me, returning to the scene of the crime. I'm an idiot."

"I'm sorry, I didn't mean to upset you, I just—we're single now. Can't we just enjoy ourselves?"

I start feeling around in the grass for my purse. "Sure. That would be great if we could leave it just at that, but how likely do you think that is? It's time, Beck. Settle down with Amanda or another local girl. Stop holding out for me."

"Is that what you think I'm doing?"

"Here we are on the grass with your hand on my breast, trying to get me into bed. You wouldn't be doing that if you were serious about anyone. Have you had a single girlfriend since the divorce?"

His silence is my answer. With a last explosion and an appreciative roar from the crowd, the fireworks end.

"Don't make me responsible for your loneliness. You're free, okay? Move on, Beck. It's well past time."

Finally I snag the handle of my purse, slip my feet back into my shoes, and trot through the grass back to the glowing torch lights of the party tent, as the rest of the crowd files up the stairs. When my mother and Al catch up to me near a hanging lantern, Mom's eyes go wide. "Honey! You're crying, what's wrong?"

So I am, as it turns out. "Tough memories here, Mom. I shouldn't have come."

"I'm sorry, I should never have asked you. I'd have thought five years... C'mon, let's get you home. Where's your sweater?"

"I dropped it, I guess. It's too dark to look. Leave it."

I allow her to lead me by the hand to the car, where Al climbs into the back without being asked. He's such a considerate, good man. I hope my mom doesn't let him slip away for something as pointless as nameless fear.

Before my mom starts the car, she hands me a tissue from her purse. "For fixing your makeup, dear. You're a bit smudged."

I flip down the visor and open the mirror. Not only has my mascara run, but my lipstick is smeared all over my face.

CHAPTER 6

Beck
Thursday, July 4, 2013

AS I REJOIN THE LANTERN-LIT CIRCLE OF THE PARTY, MY father sees me first, shakes his head, and turns away.

I look down to see what it is about me that's disappointed him this time. That's when I realize: I'm carrying Anna's sweater. I found it when I was putting my shoes back on, picking up her wine glass and my beer bottle. I didn't want anyone to break the glass and cut themselves in the dark.

He thinks he's figured it all out. Except he hasn't, of course. Part of me wants to march right up and explain that Anna, whom he seems to think wants to get her hooks in me permanently, has in fact thrown me over for good.

But I won't get back into his favor, anyway, so I give it up and decide what I want more than anything is another beer. And maybe two or eight more.

I go back over the last few minutes in my mind, reliving my latest stupidity. It all started so well. On the hill, in the fading light, she had never looked more beautiful and serene. Anna had been leaning back on her hands, with her long legs crossed. Her thin dress outlined her breasts, and her skirt hiked up her thigh. Then she lay down on her sweater as the sun vanished and the dark obscured us. I took a risk and reached for her fingers. She let me take her hand, and I felt this little jump in my chest.

Her body was so familiar; soft and warm as ever. She seemed relaxed, even eager, as I kissed her. I was young again, like all the intervening years and disasters had dried up like dew in the sun... But of course she wouldn't go back in the house with me; the moment carried me away or I'd never have asked. We're not sixteen. Our old mistakes rear up over and over to remind us how careless and stupid we've been.

I've almost made it to the tent when I hear her voice.

"Where were you? I was looking all over for you before the..." Amanda trails off when she notices the sweater in my hand, and the glass and bottle in my other. She looks fixedly at my face, then without a word reaches into her purse for a tissue. "Here," she says, her voice flat and her eyes narrow. "You've got lipstick on you."

My hands are full, so I stand there like an idiot as she mops me up.

"Amanda..." I have no followup, though.

"It's fine, Will. We weren't exclusive or anything. I just wish you'd told me how much you were carrying a torch, you know? Would have saved me some trouble. I mean, that's what people said, but you know small towns. I thought it was just a B.S. rumor. I mean, really. Five years? And like what, twenty years before that? You really are stuck on her."

I've finally sidled over to a round table and deposited the glass and beer. I place the sweater over the back of a folding chair, as if that's Anna's seat and she'll be right back.

"It was just for old time's sake. It didn't mean anything."

God, I'm a rotten liar. And Amanda knows it. She just shakes her hair back and rolls her eyes. "I'll bring the ad copy to Paul. Probably makes more sense I talk to him from now on. See ya."

She turns on a heel and strides off into the throng, ignoring my dad, who tries to stick a hand out to shake hers.

The only beer left is Bud Light, but I don't really care by now. I grab one and plop down in a rented folding party chair, nearly tipping over backwards in the soft grass. The night air is cooler, but the humidity of July still presses in. My chest feels heavy, like it's hard to draw in a deep breath.

It's Amy who sits down next to me, and for this I'm glad. She's never been one to judge.

"So. Word gets around. You and Anna a thing now?"

"Not hardly. We were having a nostalgic moment, let's say. And anyway, what, a little lipstick on my face and suddenly I'm going to marry her or something?"

"Easy there. I only said 'a thing' not 'engaged' or even 'dating'. Hey, you're racing through that beer pretty fast."

"I think I'll just stay the night."

"Probably wise. Fireworks traffic is hell, and anyway—"

"Anyway, what?"

"Nothing."

She's looking away from me. I know what she was going to say. Anyway, what do I have to go home for? Not a goddamn thing is what.

"So, where's Paul?"

"He went in the house with Penelope." An expression passes over her face I can't quite read.

"Are you guys okay?"

She picks at her thumbnail, frowning as if in deep concentration. "Oh, *we* are. I mean, we're not fighting, nothing like that. But this whole thing we're going through…" Amy lets the sentence trail off into the night. "I've been let down so many times, I'm starting to cut to the chase and go straight to the worst."

The Amy I knew best, the newly thin Amy, engaged to Paul, used to have cheerful slogans pinned up around her house, the kinds of things on kitschy motivational posters, but she reveled in them with a charming lack of irony. Her half-full glass had a silver lining and her sun was always coming out tomorrow.

I pat her arm in as brotherly a way as I can manage. We don't have much chance to be affectionate, Amy and me.

Amy sits up straighter and forces a smile. "Well, maybe you should get busy on some more nieces and nephews."

"I'm old, too. Call Tabatha and get her on the job."

"Doesn't matter how old the men are. Amanda is fresh as a daisy."

"And done with me. She saw the lipstick on my face and leapt to a conclusion about me and Anna."

Amy rolls her eyes and stretches out her arms overhead. "Ah, that's the trouble with the young. Always making rash decisions."

Paul spots us and charges across the grass. "Hey, honey," he says, ignoring me, his mushy grin only for his wife. He takes her hands and pulls her up. "Pen fell asleep inside and Mom is going to keep an eye on her here tonight. Let's get out of here, what do you say?"

Finally, a smile lights her up, and I recognize the Amy I have always known. My brother waves to me before spiriting her away and it occurs to me, watching them go, that he's a better husband than I ever was.

CHAPTER 7

Anna
Friday, July 5, 2013

WE'VE PICKED UP MOM'S DRESS, FRESHLY CLEANED AND pressed, and hung it on the back of a door in the sewing room. It had been Cami's bedroom as a girl, and she painted it sunny yellow in that last vicious summer living with her father.

Even behind the plastic of the garment bag, the dress is lovely.

"Lunch?" Mom asks brightly.

"No. Not lunch. A talk, instead."

I sit down on a futon against the far wall, facing her Bernina sewing machine, one of the last relics from her life with my dad. It had been a gift from him, both perfect and horribly wrong because they couldn't afford it.

"Have you talked to Al about how you feel about the house?"

My mom slumps against the back of the futon. "Yes."

"Oh, good. And?"

"And nothing's changed. He can't move in here. He just absolutely feels he can't, and in fact he was upset that I didn't say something earlier. He wonders what else I haven't been telling him."

A thread of a crack runs through her voice and she tugs at a curl.

"So what are you going to do?"

She looks around the room, and I know in her mind's eye, she's seeing the rest of the house, as lovingly restored first by Cami and then by herself as tenant.

"I'll probably marry him."

"Probably? I hope that's not what you said to him."

"No, goodness. I told him I would get used to the new house. And he promised I could take my time moving in, and he'd help me move as many plants from my garden as would survive the transfer."

"So where does 'probably' come in?"

My mother angles toward me on the futon, but her eye is on the sapphire engagement ring she turns around and around on her finger. "I'm worried that part of me is just getting married because he asked, because I didn't want to be a burden to you, and don't you dare object, Anna Geneva. A single, aging mother hundreds of miles away from where you live is a burden even if my blood pressure is good and it isn't always.

"And here we come down to it. Leaving this house and moving in with him and suddenly I'm his wife? I haven't been a wife, not really, in so many years. I'm not sure I know how to do it anymore. I never knew! With Robert, I felt most of the time like his nagging older sister, or heaven help me, even his mother. Always telling him he was in the wrong."

"He always was in the wrong."

"Being right was cold comfort, especially when he left me, left us. Alone."

"Al won't be like that."

"I know he won't, but I feel how I feel. Is it normal to be this terrified?"

"I wouldn't know firsthand, but look, you're not a naïve little ingénue who thinks that marriage is a lifetime of sunset walks on the beach. Of course you've got worries. But Al is not Robert Geneva, and thank God for that."

I stare hard at her face, trying to discern from her minute expression changes if I've gotten through to her at all.

"Well." She dusts off her hands as if she's been working. "Speaking of the beach. Let's get some lunch and go. I feel like a swim."

As my body nestles into the sand, I decide there is no single sensation better than the warm July sun drying cool drops of Lake Michigan off of my skin.

Okay, maybe there's one that's better. But this is number two.

The rhythmic rushing of the waves punctuated by the shrieks of gulls and children—with my eyes closed, I can't tell which—casts me back to the best times of my life here in Haven. If only I could bottle this up and take it home with me to Chicago, and I could open it up in the grinding gray gloom of February, or for that matter, sunny July days when I'm stuck at the computer or in court.

As I heave a contented sigh that seems to empty me out from my scalp to my soles, I realize how seldom I have reason to exhale like this.

I detect a snore next to me, where my mother lies prone, her hat over her face and SPF 50 on the rest of her. She's only dipped her feet in the lake so far.

My cell phone buzzes on the towel. Oh jeez, is Michelle in crisis again? But no, it's Cami. My voice is bright with my smile as I pick up. "Hey, preggo!"

"Can't call me that anymore, yeah?"

"Oh congratulations! Really?"

"Yes really. I'll text you a pic in a minute of Mr. Graham. We named him that because it rhymes with my mom's name and we liked it better than Stan. We're already calling him Graham Cracker and talking about how we want to eat him. I never knew that was literal, Anna. I do kinda want to eat him. Do I sound insane? I think it's the lack of sleep. That'll last a while, so they tell me."

Hot tears quiver in my lashes. Cami deserves this so much after the start in life she had. "I know you wish your mom could be here."

"And my dad, too, believe it or not."

"I do believe it."

Cami starts cooing to the baby and I can feel this huge dopey grin unfurl on my face. Hard-edged, laconic Cami and she's cooing and everything.

"There, Hank took him. Aww, he's going to change his butt for me. What a guy. So tell me, Anna, how's Haven? And the house and the bride-to-be and all of it? Tell me quick before I get sucked back into Babyland, never to return. Did you do it with Beck yet? You going to smuggle him back home in your trunk?"

"Of course not."

"If you say so. Ooh, the Graham Cracker is hungry. Here comes the boob! Sorry, that was TMI. Meant to hang up first. I'll text a pic when he's not sucking on my nipple. See you back home!"

I tuck my phone back under my wadded-up T-shirt and sigh now for a different reason. Home, which means lawsuits and clients and emergencies from Poor Divorcing Michelle and the apartment that had been feeling cozy but here on this bright and windy beach seems like a dark cubbyhole. Cami's there, but then she won't be there for me, not the way she used to. I've watched it again and again with my friends who procreate, without bitterness but with some sadness as parenthood enveloped them. Sure, I could rescue them for happy hour sometimes, or stop over for a quick drink on the balcony while the husband is conned into supervising the brood. But they've crossed a border and they will never be back on this side, with me.

"God, I don't want to go back," I say, to myself really, and throw my arm up over my eyes.

"So don't." My mom's voice is muffled somewhat by her hat. "And congrats to Cami."

"Eavesdropper. Anyway, I have work when I get back. I haven't won the lottery."

"You know, Anna, sometimes it's okay for a job to be just a job. I like sewing at Agatha's but is that my life's mission? Hemming prom dresses and letting out seams for bridesmaids who can't leave the potato chips alone?"

"It's my own practice. I've spent five years building it up and learning to do my own paperwork and—"

"You spent that long and more trying to make partner and you got off that treadmill at the last minute. And now you work just as hard, don't you? For less money, too."

"I like my job." I prop up on my elbows and lift my mother's hat off her face. She flinches in the glare and turns over. "You want me back here, don't you? That's why you're trying to get me to quit."

"Who's trying? You're the one who said you didn't want to go back."

"It's vacation. I said this same thing in Cancun once but I didn't mean it."

My mom turns her head on her folded arms, facing me. She looks so young like this, stretched out on her towel with her floppy hat, her pink plastic flip flops in the sand by her head. "I do worry about you. Whenever you call, you're calling from work, or pausing your work at home. I almost never hear you talk about friends, or hobbies, or men. But the other thing is I don't hear you really fired up about your work. You used to love the law. Remember how you'd recount to me an exhausting debate in one of your classes over some fine constitutional point? Or you'd call me all pumped up with a victory that I probably wouldn't understand either, in your Miller Paulson days? If your work filled you up I wouldn't care, but it doesn't seem to."

"You just said your work can be just a job."

"If you have a life outside your work, that's true."

"Poor spinster Anna, is it? Et tu, Mom?"

"That's a cheap shot. I'm not doing 'poor spinster' with you. I'm just worried."

"I promise you, I'm doing fine."

"And is 'fine' all you want?"

"What if it is?" I flop down on the sand flat again, closing my eyes against the searing disk of the sun, which just minutes before had seemed like such a balm.

I can hear my mother sitting up and rearranging. I throw my arm over my face again. The haloes of the sun swim around in the darkness behind my lids. She says, "You know, you once told me that I was brave, in a way, to have tried to reunite with your father."

"That doesn't sound like me." I was either quietly furious or shrieking back then, livid that my mother would be so foolish after years of abandonment.

"I remember it distinctly because it was so unlike everything else you said all summer. You said, 'Maybe you were the braver one for daring to hope out loud.'"

"I must have been delirious."

"You were both right and wrong, I think. It wasn't hope, or courage, that tempted me to let your father back in my life. It was fear. All those years, I never dared to become anything other than Robert's wife. I'd given up any hope of a career of my own, I gave up a relationship with my family when I eloped. I rotted away in that store, wearing my ring under my shirt, never dating anyone, aging behind the counter. It was all out of fear that I didn't know how to be anyone else. On the other hand, it indeed was a kind of crazy hope to think I could be happy again with him. I think anyone who gets married at all has that kind of hope. It's insane, if you think about it, that you pledge to spend the rest of your life with someone no matter what. Yet people do it every single day. Even old ladies like me."

"Maybe I'm not wired that way."

"Wiring, my skinny freckled behind. You're not a machine."

"You have a freckled behind? News to me."

"You're changing the subject, Counselor."

"Oh, God, don't call me that. I hate that."

My mother falls silent, letting the waves and the gulls and the splashing fill the air instead.

Then she asks—quietly, almost speaking to herself—"Is there anything you hope for, Anna?"

It surprises me that I can't answer her.

Back at the house, I almost knock my mother down in the driveway because I'm distracted by the picture Cami texted me of her new baby. She'd taken the photo selfie-style with one outstretched arm and so her radiant face and the baby's scrunched sleeping face are in the frame.

My mom is stock-still in the driveway, staring at something in her hand. I stash my phone and realize it's a postcard. She shakes her head and hands it to me before stomping her way up the drive.

It's a Chicago postcard with the Buckingham Fountain on the front. My dad's scrawl on the back reads:

Dear Maeve,

I am happy for you that you finally found someone to take care of you. I hope he treats you right. If my travels so permit, I might stop by to wish you well, but I promise that's all I have on my mind. It's hard to believe but I never stopped caring about you and that's still true even though you'll be someone else's wife.

Yours,
Robert

My mom has already stomped her way into the house and left the door open behind her. I can hear her muttering and slamming before I even cross the threshold.

"Go ahead!" she shouts back from the kitchen. "Go ahead and tell me you were right about telling him about the wedding."

"The thought never crossed my mind." Well, I wasn't going to say it out loud, anyway. "If it's any consolation, it's probably just another big plan that will never come to fruition like all the rest. Anyway it's not like you gave him the exact location. Watch him stop in every church in the county looking for you, when you'll be on the beach."

"I'm so foolish. Al's going to be upset."

"Are you sure?" I drop my beach bag on the floor and join her in the kitchen, leaning on the counter next to her, our ankles crossed. We often do this, accidentally mirror each other. "It doesn't seem like much gets to him."

"Robert gets to him. In fact…"

She trails off, staring at her feet.

"In fact what, Mom?"

"He wondered if part of the reason I don't want to move is so that I don't stop getting the postcards."

"Oh, no." I'm tempted to challenge her: is that, in fact, the real reason? Even a little? But I don't dare add to her agitation. I fear for her blood pressure. "So, what did you say?"

"I said that was nonsense and how dare he

think that? But we smoothed it over some, so I think it's okay."

"Mom, I truly don't think he'll show up. He just wants to stoke his ego by imagining he can still get to you. Remember how he never has two quarters to rub together and always has to rely on rides and favors from other people? Those crooks from the gambling ring for instance? Is he really going to get one of those jokers to drive him all the way here so he can spy on his ex? And if he does, well, so what? We'll get someone to haul him off if he causes the least disturbance."

"Who would do that? Who's going to be my personal bouncer?"

"Beck would," I answer without a moment's thought. "He knows the history already, right? I bet with his family being so prominent he probably knows half the cops in town. He could intervene, keep Dad busy and then call the cops. In fact just with the threat of cops and Dad would hightail it. I bet he's got warrants for this and that."

My mother smiles sadly at her feet again. "Robert Geneva always did keep things interesting. Even by postcard."

I watch a wistful look cross her face, with a ghost of a smile that could almost be fond nostalgia. She shakes her head a little, then scowls at her feet. "I need to get my nails done. A summer beach wedding and here I am with gnarly toes and nasty chipped polish."

Once I'd have argued, dragged her back to the point at hand. Today I allow her the privilege of changing the subject. "Well, we can't have that. Let's wash the sand off and go get our toes prettied up."

After I send my mom off to the shower, I pull out my phone so I can reach out to Beck. Once upon a time, I'd have swiped open the window with our running text conversation, but that was five years and a few phones ago, and anyway, I deleted that contact information long before.

There's one number I do remember, though, one number that I always know will work.

I put on my best professional lawyer voice as I dial up Becker Development. "May I speak to Will Becker, please? Yes, the younger. I'll hold." While on hold, I reread the card. *Finally found someone to take care of you.* The gall of that statement is breathtaking. My mother has never needed a man to "take care" of her. She took care of herself, and me, and eventually Aunt Sally too, for all those lonely years.

CHAPTER 8

Beck
Saturday, July 6, 2013

THE MORNING SUN WARMS THE BACK OF MY NECK AS I stroll along the pier. The beach is nearly empty, except for a man throwing a stick for his dog and a woman jogging the stretch just above the surf line, weaving with the crash of the waves, staying on the firm wet sand. Soon enough the beach will be jammed with families on the tail end of their holiday weeks, and the man would be scolded to leash his dog. But this early, the lifeguards are still asleep and it's every man for himself.

The pier walk has become my summer Saturday ritual on my weekends without the kids. Harry is so young and absent-minded, Madeline's near-drowning so stark in my memory, that I don't dare take them out to this concrete slab with no railing, treacherous rocks, and roiling water all around. So this is what I do, part pleasure, part penance.

I didn't have a choice, really, but to agree to let the kids stay with Sam and their grandparents. I should have guessed this would be the outcome, what with July 4 being on a Thursday, and their planned long drive home on Friday. It only seemed natural that Sam would ask to swap weekends so she could extend their grandparent time. And what was I supposed to say? What would my children have said if I insisted they leave Grandma and Grandpa Chapman's house just to come sit in my duplex? Sure I'd take them to the beach, but they are Haven kids and have been to the beach a million times. Grandma and Grandpa Chapman were primed to spoil them silly for three more days and no kid would swap that for boring old Dad who doesn't have a big enough yard for a swing set.

When my kids heard of the change in plans, they roared a great cheer and I flinched.

I reach the end of the pier and lower myself to sitting. The waves over the breakwater are hypnotic, the water at this distance looks nearly jade green.

I'd just hung up from that call with Samantha when the secretary put Anna's call through. Katie is new enough to think nothing of it, and for that I was grateful, though I bet if someone overheard, they soon filled her in.

I laughed at first, thinking Anna was kidding. Me, acting as security of a sort at her mother's wedding? I realized then from the tone of her voice that this was no joke.

"I don't want Mom to have to worry about it, and I don't know who else I can ask. I don't want to put a wedding guest on guard duty, I don't want to, like, hire a goon or something. I just need someone there to keep an eye out. Someone who isn't a stranger so I don't have to tell this whole stupid story again."

"Of course I will."

"I mean, hopefully you won't have to do anything but stand there and smile and then come eat cake with us. Heck, bring that Mandy girl as your date."

"Oh, well, a certain someone's lipstick all over my face put an end to that." I'd meant to say it playfully, but my tone turned dark before I could censor myself.

The silence rang loud on Anna's end. Her voice, only moments before friendly and entreating, grew cold. "I appreciate your help, Will. The wedding is at seven at Crescent Beach."

I tried to keep her on the line but she clicked off too fast. It was stupid of me to say that, as if Mandy dumping me was somehow Anna's fault; as if I even minded it. I was the one who first reached for Anna in the grass, I was the one who tried to get her into the house for sex.

"Well done, jackass," I mutter. A gull lands near me, cocking its tiny bird head in hopes I brought some food. "Sorry, this jackass didn't bring any food. Go away." The gull just stands there and shits on the pier. Some security I am. I can't even scare away an ugly bird.

On my own initiative, I show up about five p.m. to the wedding venue. This hidden sliver of beach is known mostly to locals. Havenites have been known to vandalize new, bolder signs advertising this gem, and town planning regulations were eventually written almost specifically to eliminate any possibility for signs that would be actually helpful.

Eventually, despite the unwillingness to share Crescent Beach with the outside world, the town did erect a gazebo and a covered picnic area near one end, and it's proven popular for a certain type of wedding: small affairs, often second marriages, with brides who have enough daring to risk the elements.

As Anna had explained when I called back to confirm details—her tone never wavering from cool professionalism—it seemed unlikely her father would even know where to show up, if he really did make it to Haven. He'd more likely try the Presbyterian church where they had the funeral for his sister Sally four years ago, or any other of the local churches around. "But even with that, just knowing you're coming has made Mom feel better. For that I'll always be grateful," she'd said, her phrasing bearing an odd finality, as if she never intended to see me again after today.

I tried to tell her about the seagull on the

pier but she didn't laugh. She said only "cute", in the same way Samantha used to say "right" when I told a story about work and she wasn't really listening.

She'd described her father to me, and it seemed safe that I'd be able to pick him out of the crowd, even though I had never met him. Early sixties, graying hair, distinct limp, probably shabbily dressed.

As I got ready in my townhouse, I did entertain a fantasy of somehow dramatically saving the day and Anna throwing her arms around me in gratitude. I guess even evolved, progressive men can have a knight in shining armor daydream.

I decide to seat myself in one of the folding chairs toward the back, and I angle the chair slightly so that I can see the whole venue, including gazebo and parking lot. After I've done so, I realize I have a view of the bride getting her picture taken at the water's edge. A breeze ruffles the petals of a flower wound somehow into Maeve's hair, which is piled behind her head. The same wind lifts a filmy train and it drifts like a following spirit. From this distance it doesn't take much imagination to think that's Anna standing there.

Weddings and funerals have a way of throwing one's memory back to other weddings and funerals, and today is no different. I slam the drawer hard on thoughts of my wedding to Sam. But then my mind leaps to another memory, only somewhat less awful. Amy's wedding to Paul, in which Anna got drafted to fill in for an injured bridesmaid, thrusting us together in the midst of our affair.

The way I treated her that day, having just confessed the affair to my wife, is probably the second worst thing I've ever done. The first being the affair itself.

Anna seemed optimistic that day, despite the deep awkwardness. I will never forget the way her face shifted at the moment I told her that Sam knew. She'd worn a kind of secret smile during a dance we were sharing, because she no doubt thought we could revel in that moment together with no one the wiser. Dancing at a wedding was perfectly harmless, after all. Or it would have been, if I hadn't confessed already to Sam, and lost my nerve for warning Anna.

So when I told her, that closely held pleasure melted away and her features hardened into a type of mask I'd seen before: anytime she talked of her father and wished not to lose her composure. Only that time it had been my doing. I had caused her to put on the mask.

I'd entreated her later to give me some time, but considering I was about to go back home to my wife and child, I could hardly blame her for heading back to Chicago and leaving me in my crumbling marriage.

I spot Anna as she walks to the shoreline to join her mother. She's wearing a silky knee-length dress in light green, her own red hair pulled back, with a few loose curls bouncing in the wind. She fusses with the flower in her mom's hair, then she reaches over and pulls Maeve in for a sideways embrace. They both carry simple bunches of daisies that might have been picked from someone's garden. Maybe they were, at that. Maeve does love her flowers.

Anna looks so relaxed and happy, even joyous, and this sight is all the more wondrous and poignant for being so rare. I feel buoyed by the pleasure of seeing it, then crash down again because she's going to get on a train tomorrow and be gone. For as long as Maeve is still alive and well in Haven, Anna will continue to pop back into my circumscribed orbit, shine for a few days and then vanish again. Someday, hopefully many years from now, Maeve will pass on, and Anna will never return, I feel sure of it.

The thought comes to me, almost as if someone else has spoken it into my head: *I want to make her smile like that.*

I shake my head at my own idiocy. How many chances does a man expect? My family is right, Anna is right. I should stop mooning over her and get on with my life.

I can't stop looking at her, though. Anna is so unaware of anyone and anything but the lake, her mother, and the wedding, that she has begun to twirl a piece of hair, a habit of her youth that I always loved, and she tried to break.

It's only when she happens to turn in my direction, and her face falls, that I remember my mission here. I look over my shoulder and see a man standing where a path in the woods opens up onto the sand. He's gray haired and wearing beat-up jean shorts and a faded button-down shirt so old I can't tell what the pattern might have been. But it's the expression on his face that identifies him for me. I can't think of anyone who would stare so fixedly at those two women other than Robert Geneva. I nod back toward Anna—*I got this*—and stride as quickly as the sand allows over to him.

"You're not wanted here," I tell him.

"I don't expect I am."

"Then what do you say we go for a walk? Right back to your car."

He leans against a tree, folds his arms, and makes as if to stay for a while. "I'm not going to cause any ruckus. I just want to see, is all. I just want to watch her have a real wedding for once."

I tighten my fists as indignation rises in my chest.

I can hear Anna's voice in my head as if she's beside me. *Bullshit!* she'd shout. And she'd be right. A man doesn't cross several states to just stand on the sidelines and not even try to talk to his ex.

I step closer. My voice comes out low and gravelly, and it sounds strange to my own ears. "Your being here is ruckus enough. They've spotted you and now they're upset. You don't belong here and you will not ruin their day."

It's my father's voice I'm hearing. The patriarch in charge.

Robert Geneva makes no move to leave. The

brazenness of his presence is outrageous. But that's very much in character, as Anna explained. He never let a little thing like reality interrupt a scheme of his.

He cackles, coughs, and spits a wad of phlegm onto the sandy trail. "You gonna punch a rickety old man with a bad hip?"

"You think anyone would care if I did?" His arrogance plucks a string in me. As a father, and one-time husband, I know well the enormity of the agony he's caused. I've seen it play out in the pain that flashes across Anna's face before she puts on her mask. I've seen the defensive crouch in which Anna has spent most of her life expecting everyone to hurt her, leave her. And here he stands, the maestro of all that pain, wiping his nails on his shirt like a smarmy B-grade actor.

I could almost smack my fist right into that curling smirk, but that same smirk catches my attention. Sonofabitch, he's hoping I'll hit him, shove him, knock him down. He can get me hauled off for assault and ruin the wedding with the spectacle of it.

I unclench my hands and take one step back.

"You bet I'll call the cops, though. I figure you've got a warrant or two. In any case you're an unwanted person." Anna had coached me on this phrasing. I find myself hoping he'll try to push past, even hit me. Give me a reason, jackass.

Unexpectedly, he turns to retreat down the trail. I follow him, because for all I know he could loop through the woods and come back out on a different spot of beach. It occurs to me I may end up babysitting this joker until the vows are accomplished.

"Maybe I'll just give you a note for Anna. You her boyfriend?"

"No."

"No? Why the hell not?"

He's leading back toward a trailhead at a parking lot further down the road. Thank God Anna asked me to help: I shudder to think of her walking down this isolated trail with this guy, father or not. "What do you mean 'why the hell not'?"

"You were staring at her like she's the goddamn love of your life."

"You don't know anything."

"I was standing there watching before any of y'all took notice. Maeve kept waving at her man. Least, I assume that was him in the gray suit. And Anna was looking so pretty in green, she always did, too. Matches her eyes, like that poem her mom used to quote all the time. By whatshisnose. 'Nature's first green is gold...'"

"Robert Frost. 'Nothing Gold Can Stay'."

"Heh. Damn right old Frosty. Nothing gold. Ah, don't bother with women anyway, young man. Nothing gold can stay and nothing silver, or copper, or even goddamn tin." He stops in the path, where it's by now packed dirt strewn with pine needles. He turns to me. "Maeve isn't the only one who moved on. I got a new lady, had more kids. We were together for twenty years if you can believe it and she ran off with somebody else. Some asshole with a big stupid house. And people that stay together don't stay in their gold, either. They're just too lazy to do anything about it and just get more and more ornery, side by side. If Maeve and this new guy make it, it'll be because one of them kicks off before they get tired of each other."

"Keep walking," I tell him. "To hell with you."

"Suit yourself. What's your game plan, Boy Wonder? It's a free country and I can breathe in Haven if I damn well want."

"I don't care where you breathe as long as it's not here. Stay away or I'm calling the cops."

We emerge from the trailhead into a small parking area covered with bark chips. He leans back against a rusty Ford Escort. "Seems to me the bride and groom wouldn't appreciate the sirens and fuss."

"No, they wouldn't."

"So what if I go back there anyhow? You going to wrestle me to the ground? Punch me in the nose?"

It occurs to me he's angling for something. "What do you want, Mr. Geneva?" I reach for my wallet. I've got cash in here, it might be as simple as that.

He rears back a little and actually looks wounded. "You think I'm extorting you?"

"I'm just trying to get you the hell out of here. You've seen it for yourself now. She's really getting married. She doesn't want to see you. I won't let you make this any worse than it is already."

He turns back to the car. "Just give them a

note from me, then. Promise me that and I'll go away forever." Without waiting for a response he settles into the driver's seat, legs sticking out the door, and uses his lap for a table to scribble a note on a writing tablet he produced from somewhere inside the car.

He folds the paper so roughly it's more of a wadded-up ball than a note, and I jam it into my pocket. I don't know if I can trust his word; he might circle back the minute he's out of my sight. I will call the police as a preemptive measure. I bet a sheriff's deputy would casually drop by Crescent Beach right around seven, just to keep an eye on things. It's a small town and everyone shopped at Maeve's Nee Nance Store, got their mail delivered by Al. It's the kind of thing Havenites will do for one another. As Robert Geneva slams the door and the car coughs to life and sputters away, I use my cell phone to take a picture of the license plate.

On my long trudge on the dark path back toward the wedding, I shake my head anew at the balls of this guy to show up at his discarded wife's new wedding day, adding yet another stupid stunt to his long list of catastrophic mistakes.

"Some people never learn," I mutter, my only audience being the cool piney woods. Then I laugh darkly. I ought to know.

CHAPTER 9

Anna
Saturday, July 6, 2013
The Wedding

THE AISLE, IF IT COULD BE CALLED THAT, IS RATHER SHORT, seeing as we have only about twenty-five chairs. So, to give the high school quartet enough time to get through some bars of Pachelbel's Canon in D, Mom and I are starting almost back in the woods for our long trip across the sand, up the gazebo steps, to stand next to Al.

And it is in this way that I'm giving away my mother to the man who loves her, who probably loved her quietly all those years; a decade he spent buying Snickers and Diet Coke at her little ramshackle store. Sunny, cheerful Al, who turned out to be excellent at biding his time.

We'd decided just to walk next to each other with our flowers, but now that seems silly, so I extend my hand and she takes it, having to slip hers into mine because she's shorter. I therefore feel like I'm leading her, steadying her, over the uneven sand, and maybe I am. I was prepared to always be the one to steady her, even if she thought of herself as a burden.

This trip across the sand is taking longer than we thought. We didn't practice this in the casual and rushed rehearsal, not thinking a beach wedding needed very much fuss.

Al looks unruffled, so whatever the last conversation they had about my mother moving in, he must be satisfied. Or maybe he's faking it, who can tell? Maybe he's about to throw up.

I squeeze Mom's hand and turn my head to smile at her, but her gaze is locked straight ahead, distant, as if on the horizon. Her solemnity makes me worry. I quickly search the rows of chairs and see Beck. He nods to me, and nods back at the woods, letting me know he's paying attention, he's watching. I'm sure my mother is afraid my dad will suddenly materialize for some grand and pointless gesture. I can't help but wonder if a tiny part of her, the fossilized remnant of her love for my father, is hoping he might.

I doubt it will happen, because I trust Beck to take care of it. He said so, in our whispered conference after he returned from the woods. He said he'd keep my dad away, and Beck doesn't lie to me. He doesn't make promises he can't keep, either, which is why he was honest with me five years ago. Many men in his position would have spun whatever lies were necessary to keep me in Haven, waiting, like a flopping fish on a line. I'm reminded now what a painful gift that honesty was.

We melt through the few rows of chairs and pick our careful way up the gazebo steps, Mom having to drop my hand to pick up her dress. We are wearing nice flat sandals, all the easier for walking in the sand. Al had campaigned to go barefoot, but it's a wood gazebo and there are slivers.

Al's brother Dale stands next to him, a version of the groom with darker hair and a bushier moustache. With my mother there's just me. Out in the crowd are Mom and Al's Haven friends, with whom they raise a glass at the Tip-a-Few on more than a few Friday nights. Grant and Veronica, mom's oldest friends, sit in the center of the front row, all sappy smiles. Mom's relatives are all far away, or dead, and so this small crowd here represents the whole of Mom's sphere and mine, too, when I'm in town. It steadies me to know Beck is out there, and not just because he's keeping my wayward father at bay.

As the minister clears her throat to draw our attention, I steal a look over my shoulder. There might be a dark figure in the woods, but I think that's my imagination, because I blink and it's gone. I do see Beck. He gives me a sad smile and then looks down, as if he doesn't have the right to hold my gaze.

"Welcome, one and all, as we celebrate the wedding of Maeve Callahan Geneva and Albert Louis Landry."

We move through the steps of this brief wedding, rapidly approaching the big moment, and I keep stealing glances at my mother's face. She looks grave, still. It is serious business to get married, but she picked a beach gazebo and a hippie female minister in deliberate opposition to a sonorous churchy proceeding.

Even Al's sunny composure looks a little ruffled as he tries to catch his bride's eye, but her gaze seems to only go from the minister to the lake vista behind her.

"Do you, Maeve, take this man..."

My mother begins to fidget, shifting her weight back and forth. I am by now holding both bunches of flowers, and Mom has been prompted to face Al, so I can no longer see her expression. I can only see Al's concern and guess what she looks like. Pale, worried. Mom also blinks a lot when she's distressed.

Al breaks the script. He drops my mother's hands and steps into her, wrapping her into an embrace. The minister is thrown for a moment and trails off, then she quips, "I guess he just can't wait" and the audience breaks into giggles. I know they couldn't have detected my mom's anxiety from back there in the sand. Only the few of us up here on these weatherworn and slivered wood slats realize what's going on. He's loving her through it. Whatever is causing her to be so worried right now, he's gathering her up, saying *I've got you.* My tears start rolling.

I loathe public crying, but today I don't bother to look skyward and blink the tears away.

Al steps back and nods to the minister. The minister resumes the vows, and my mother has stopped her shifting.

"I will," Mom finally declares, in a voice clear and strong. When Al gets his chance, he booms it loud, like a ringmaster or something, prompting more chuckles. He sneaks a look at me, and winks. He's saying it to me, too. I'm suddenly and surprisingly glad I have a stepfather.

At "You may kiss the bride," I can't help but look back at the woods. This would be the most outrageous moment for Robert Geneva to appear, but all seems calm. Beck nods to me when he catches my eye. Then the high school quartet strikes up their chamber music version of the recessional and they're off down the steps. In the sand, Mom and Al make a big show of kicking off their shoes, so I do, too, as does Al's brother, and most of the wedding guests happily follow suit. My toes sink into the sun-warmed sand. She did it. She got married with a smile, and never even saw my reprobate father. I could faint with relief.

CHAPTER 10

Anna
Saturday, July 6, 2013

INSTEAD OF A RECEIVING LINE, THE GUESTS ARE JUST crowding around, waiting for their turn to give their good wishes. I toy with my daisies and hang back, because I'll get my private moments with my mother later.

Beck approaches, and he extends his arms half-heartedly, like he's afraid I'll decline his hug. Of course I won't, not after what he's done today, after what he's meant to me all these years. He's a good egg, after all. He's no more flawed than any of us.

"You look beautiful," he says when I step back. I glance down at the dress. Halter style top, knee length, a pretty pale green. Mom let me pick it out via pictures emailed from Agatha.

"I do clean up nice for weddings." I bite my lip

and cringe, pretending it's a squint in the setting sun. Our past has littered our conversation with landmines. "So, coming with us to our very fancy reception in the tent?" I point over my shoulder at the white tent in the sand with chairs, tables, some munchies, and an ordinary sheet cake. Mom didn't want some towering confection to get covered with blowing sand or knocked over in transit across the beach. The food is simple, almost comically so. Bacon-wrapped weenies on toothpicks, that kind of thing. There will be a tub with beer and fruity Seagram's wine coolers and a box of chardonnay sits in a tray of ice. "You've got to have yourself a plastic cup of Korbel before you go."

"Sure. Anyway, I'm still acting in my capacity as so-called security. We got Maeve married off peacefully, but you never know."

"I spy a sheriff's car in the parking lot. Has that been here the whole time?"

"Well, look at that. I do believe you're right." Beck winks at me.

"I'll invite him over. I'm sure he can't have booze right now but he could grab a piece of cake, have some punch."

"Anna, can I tell you something?"

"Not if it's serious. I'm too worn out for serious."

Beck falls silent and stares at the sand.

"Oh, fine. Do serious."

"No, this isn't a good day…"

"There never is a good day. Really, go ahead and tell me."

"Being here today reminds me of Amy and Paul's wedding."

I look away from Beck to hide my expression.

Beck clears his throat. "I know. I was an asshole. I never apologized for it. It was wrong on every level."

"I know we were wrong. You were married."

"No, listen. I wronged *you*. That's what I'm trying to say. Not just my wife. I wronged you, too. That one night it was raw emotion, for both of us. But later, with all the texting, leaving you the book, yet the whole time I was going along with Sam as if nothing was changing. I was careless with you. I'm sorry."

"It's okay. Well, it's not okay, but I don't have the words for accepting apologies on that scale. Anyway, I knew you were sorry without you saying so. I gave you that much credit."

"More than I deserved."

The crowd around my mother is thinning as they amble over to the tent, but now the photographer has the happy couple together, frolicking and kicking water at each other. Beck stands beside me and watches them. Al seizes Mom and flings her into his arms, dolllike, and plants one on her. God, I hope the photographer grabbed that shot. Everyone should be loved like that, and everyone should have a photo like that, too, for the days when love doesn't come so easy.

Al sets her down and pantomimes having hurt his back. Mom whacks him with her flowers, and daisy petals spray into the lake breeze.

"God, they're so happy," says Beck. "It's too bad they had to wait so long to find each other."

"And yet I'm sure Al would have preferred his wife never got sick and died in the first place."

"Oh, I'm sorry. I didn't know he was a widower."

"I'm just saying that it couldn't have been any other way. If Mom had divorced my father immediately she'd have dated people, maybe remarried someone else, then when Al's wife passed and he was ready to love again, Mom wouldn't have been there. Or maybe Al's wife never got sick, like I said, which would have been the best, obviously. I'm sure Mom believes that, too. And what would have been best for Mom, come to think, is if Dad had lived up to everything he was supposed to be. No one wants to be abandoned, no matter how well it works out a quarter-century later. I'm glad we can't wish our lives into something else. We might wish away something great without meaning to."

"Like my kids. If I wished away my marriage to Sam, I'd never have had Madeline or Harry. I can't imagine living without them."

"And now look. Mom and Al have made something happy out of their own tragedies."

Beck takes my shoulders and turns me gently to him. My back is to the sun but he's squinting into it. His expression is nearly painful in fact, with the full force of the evening summer rays striking him.

I interrupt him. "Wait. Let's get in the shade, what do you say?"

"No, please, don't wait. I don't want to wait. Waiting is...I love you. Still do, always did."

He spits it out rapidly, like a kid blurting out lines in the school play. He jams his hands in his pockets and stares down, avoiding the glare and probably my expression.

"Beck...that's sweet, but..."

"I know. My kids, Chicago. But why can't we figure it out somehow? Look at your mom and Al, and all they went through to get where they are."

The photographer has left them now, and they are taking a moment on the beach, as the rest of the party has now convened in the shade, around the drinks and food. They're swaying together in the breaking waves, ignoring their wet clothes and potential sunburn and whatever else there is.

Beck grabs for my hand. "We'll do Skype and text if that's all I get. I'll put a million miles on my car driving to Chicago every other weekend. Do you know what it's like in that stupid townhouse filled with toys when my kids aren't there?"

"I'm not a placeholder."

"Everyone else holds *your* place. I fill my days with people, but no matter how pretty the girl, no matter how important the business people, even my family... The only people who fill that hollow space are my kids and you, Anna. Not because you're a distraction. Because you're the only woman I want to be with. Every day, or whatever I can get. I'm tired of pretending I'm over you. We're too old to pretend, isn't that what you said? I'm terrible at it, anyway."

My heart jitters along and I feel sweaty and faint. Must we do this again? How many times, how many ways, do I have to tell him it's impossible, before he believes me?

"I can't possibly be that special that I'm holding your attention for twenty-five years. You're wavering and sad and nostalgic."

"Dammit you are that special." He's loud enough that people in the tent have turned to stare. He steps closer, lowering his voice. "You always were. I was just too pathetic to stand up for you. So I'm making my stand. You've got me, always. No matter how far away you are. It's as simple as that."

I sink into the nearest folding chair and drop my daisies on the sand. I would love things to be simple; if only they could be. Beck crouches down and picks up my flowers, then hands them to me from that position, kneeling on the sand. I have to look away from his open, hopeful face, waiting for an answer I can't give him.

My mother, genuinely tipsy, is one of the most hilarious sights I've ever witnessed. She keeps folding at the waist to laugh at everything, tipping her glass out onto the beach, where her drink splashes into little dark dots trailing her as she goes.

Neither Al nor Mom are the types to be interested in some splashy tropical vacation or a cruise ship, so they have booked an inn down in Saugatuck, which is really just a stone's throw from here, and they only plan to stay the weekend, at that.

I catch Al at the cake table with frosting in his moustache as Mom's shrieking laugh peals across the sand. "So, do I have to drive you two drunken lovebirds to your honeymoon?"

Al swallows his gob of cake. "Not unless you can get drunk on sugar. I laid off after the champagne toast. Your mother never cuts loose much, so why not?"

"She might fall asleep on the way there at this rate."

"Eh, we'll make up for it tomorrow." He elbows me and winks.

For that, I have no words.

Someone has produced a laptop and music is blaring from the tinny speakers. Disco, from the sounds of it, which was never my mother's thing but she's getting her boogie shoes on anyway, along with several other tipsy baby boomers. The sun is gone now, and I'm feeling chilly in my dress. I hadn't realized the party would go so late. I figured once the sun set and our official rental of this strip of beach was over, the newlyweds would motor off and I'd be loading leftover cake into the car. As it is, the table rental people have arrived and are starting to fold things up under here.

My mother calls, "Al! Get your ass over here!" and now it's my turn to fold in half, laughing. My mother never swears. She barely says "butt," preferring "derriere" and "rear end" and other gentle euphemisms.

I sit on one of the folding chairs the tent people haven't spirited away yet, and watch my mother and new stepfather.

After Beck ambushed me with his love declaration, my mother swooped over to me, her arms open to wrap me in a sandy, damp hug. Beck slunk away then with only a quick nod to my mother in response to her shouted "thank you!" for his guard duty. I've seen him here and there since, sipping a bottled water and roving around the periphery.

"Miss? I need to start packing these up. Sorry, but the party was over an hour ago, technically."

The burly man with stubble on his chin looks tired and I feel guilty for this party keeping all these guys out late. I stand up and relinquish the chair, noticing that the guests are finally saying their farewells. I spy a couple of cabs in the parking lot: good, someone arranged for rides for the tipsy ones. That was probably Beck, too.

I decide to go looking for him, to thank him once again for all his help today. No matter how awkward it will be, I owe him that, and I can hardly avoid him like a middle schooler who thinks he has cooties.

The moon is up by now, a nice big juicy one, so that once my eyes adjust to the dark, it's not even that hard to see. I spot him off by the woods, and jog a little in the sand to catch up, though I twist my ankle a bit and have to hop a few steps.

It's only when I get right up on him that I realize he's far too short to be Beck.

"Dad?"

"I didn't bother nobody."

I sigh. Technically this is true. A lot of what my dad always said was technically true.

"Leave her alone. She's deliriously happy and she doesn't need your bullshit. I thought Beck and the deputy chased you off." I scowl at this; I thought Beck would make sure...

"Oh don't be mad at him, Anna Banana. He's why I stayed in the trees. I'd have loved to sit right down in a chair like a proper guest and raise a toast."

"I bet that's what you wanted."

"Can you blame me for not believing it? Twenty years my beautiful Maeve waited for me. Guess I thought she'd give me a few years more."

"She told you last time you came back not to bother again. God, you never listen to anyone, do you?"

"You sound like my wife."

"Which one?"

He holds his hands up like I've got a gun on him. "Fine, fine. Guilty as charged." He folds his arms and for a moment his conniving, slick charm fades away and I see heartbreak written in his bent posture and downcast gaze.

"I thought maybe she was kinda hoping I'd come get her, which was why she told me the date. Thought maybe I could save her from marrying some boring old geezer. But she sure didn't look like she wanted saving. 'Cept from me, I guess. So, anyhow. Hey, did that fellow catch up to you yet?"

"Who, Beck? We talked. Why?"

"Nothing. Never mind. Well. I'll get out of your hair, honey. I'll write next time I'm near Chicago and my hotshot attorney daughter can buy me lunch."

I want to scream at him to go away, scream at him to stay and talk to me for one damn second about something real, but it's all futile so I agree that sure, I'll buy him lunch.

And with that he shuffles off onto the bark chip path, swallowed up by the dark woods.

"Geez, some bodyguard I turned out to be."

I jump and whirl around to see Beck a few feet away. "How long were you there?"

"When I saw you trotting toward the woods I guessed who was out there and followed. But you looked like you had things well in hand. You've never needed much saving, Anna Geneva."

"No, I guess I haven't. But I'm glad you were there. Just in case."

"You can think of me that way. As a just-in-case guy. I won't mind." Beck jumps as if someone shocked him. "Oh! I have something."

He roots through his pockets and produces a piece of crumpled paper. "Your dad gave me this. Said it's for you and your mom. It's how I got him to go away, by promising to hand this over."

I'm glad it's dark enough that Beck can't see my hand shaking as I accept the paper. Here, in my hand, is what my dad wanted to tell my mother and me, what he'd come all this way to say. It could be an apology, a real one. It could be that he wants to get to know me through more than just postcards and a promised lunch that will never materialize. It could be the way I get to know my dad before he dies, because I don't actually want him to, no matter what drifts through my brain in angry moments.

I look back toward the woods. He could be there, just a few strides away. He can't have gotten far with that limp of his.

I turn instead toward the beach, then start an uneven, wavering jog through the sand toward the water, skirting away from the party. I hear Beck catch up to me, puffing slightly. "Anna?"

The revelers don't notice us as we keep beyond the remaining party lights.

At the water's edge, the lake licks my toes and rolls back like a puppy playing games. It's rocky here, and it's easy for me to find a stone even though a cloud has passed over the moon and the dark has resurged. I jam the rock into the center of the ball of paper, then fling it with as much strength as I can muster. In the black-blue dark, I can only hear the splash. I picture the rock sinking, Lake Michigan eating away at the cheap paper, blurring the ink.

Beck reaches for my hand, but I reflexively step to the side and fold my arms. I'm still cold, even more so in the lake breeze, which flutters my dress behind me like a little flag. Silent, we stare at the lake as the cloud passes, and the moonlight bursts free again.

Car doors slam, people are calling goodbye to one another other. In the distance I can see the last of the tables and chairs are being stacked. The twinkle lights in the tent are coming down, and nature is reclaiming her beach. I hear my mother call out, "Anna?" her voice only curious, not yet worried.

"Guess you're heading back tomorrow, now that your mom is off to her honeymoon." He clears his throat and shuffles his feet. Even in the silvery blue moonlight I can discern his longing. "I had some hope you might consider staying."

I chuckle, but my voice comes out thick and it sounds nearly like a sob. "How can you still have hope? After all I've said?"

"It's not a choice to hope or not. It's only a choice whether to say it out loud."

No wonder I've had to fight so hard to stay away from Haven, from him. I was hoping all along but trying desperately not to. My resistance melts away and instead of feeling defeat, or fear, or anything I'd imagined, I finally feel like I can breathe.

I step into Beck with my full weight, catching him by surprise enough that he staggers back before he steadies me, steadies us. We hold each other tight as if there is something trying to pull us apart, though I know that at last, there's nothing at all.

CHAPTER 11

Beck
Sunday, July 7, 2013

A GROWLY, RUMBLING THUNDER AWAKENS ME, AND I am confused about what time it is, what day it is. I roll to look at my clock and it's 6:56 a.m. Another early wake-up for me in my townhouse.

I slide out of bed and into my pants, scenting the air like a mutt. Is that...coffee?

Anna is at my kitchen table, her red hair huge in all its curly, frizzy glory. The room is dark with the gray stormy morning, but she's sitting in the circle of lamplight with a coffee cup and the newspaper like she's done this every day for our whole lives.

"Couldn't sleep?"

She beams a smile at me, puts down the paper. "The storm woke me, and then, you know, sleeping in a strange bed..."

"Not that we slept so much, did we?"

Anna's wearing my shirt from last night, her panties, and that's all. The sight is so adorable, sexy and so long-awaited I can't make up my mind whether to bawl or fist-pump.

She leans back in her chair, stretching her body long with a satisfied sigh. "This is quite a luxury, isn't it? Spending a whole night together without having to sneak around. It might, in fact, be a first for us."

I smile to consider this as I make my way to the cupboard for a mug. "True. When we were kids we were trying to pretend we were virgins—"

"—Like anyone believed that."

"No, but we all liked to make the grownups feel better. And, well..."

"Then we had our affair. We can quit dancing around it. We did it, it's over and can't be helped."

"And God, we sucked at it, didn't we?"

Anna laughs. "We did! We only actually had sex one time. If everyone was going to hate us to death we should have done it every chance we got, anywhere we could."

"My office."

"The alley behind the Nee Nance."

"The car."

"We can take that one as read."

I sit down at her elbow and take my free hand with hers. "Now we can be together like this all the time, no hiding, no sneaking."

"No giving two shits what anyone thinks."

"They'll be happy for us anyway, when they see we're happy."

Anna tries—and fails—to hide her skeptical smirk behind her coffee mug. I open my mouth to score a point for optimism, but my cell phone rings.

I snatch it up. There's only one person and one reason for a call this early on a holiday weekend Sunday.

"Sam, what's wrong?"

"Will, Harry's sick. He's got a fever that won't come down even with Tylenol and he's been throwing up all night. I'm taking him to urgent care."

"I'll drive down."

Anna stands up, tense and alert. I recognize that look. She wants to spring into action.

"No, don't. For all we know by the time you got here things would be fine. I'm just letting you know. We had a nice time until then."

"Geez, I'm sorry. Can I talk to him?"

"He doesn't feel up to it."

Anna's cell phone chimes now, and we both jump. She shoots me an apologetic look and silences it.

"What was that? Is someone else there?"

Here is where it is easy to lie, redirect the conversation. That noise could've been anything, after all.

"Will? I asked you a question."

"Yes, someone's here. I don't want to talk about it now."

"I can just about guess who it is. Having a stroll down memory lane?"

"Sam, please. Not now. Just keep me posted about Harry. If it's bad I can be down there in no time. Hell, if it's dire I could see about a flight. Hug my buddy for me, ok? Give my love to Maddie."

She sighs roughly. "Of course. I'll keep you posted."

I hang up and give Anna the update on Harry, and she settles back into her chair, her expression fading from alarm to thoughtful concern.

"I'm sorry he's sick. And I'm also sorry about the phone. I thought I'd turned the sound off. It was just a client email."

"Real life barges in."

"It always does."

Thunder fills our silence, all our giddy buoyance wafting away.

"So. She didn't seem happy about you having company."

"No. But she'll have to get over it. My life is mine. No amount of punishment, from myself or Sam, is ever going to make her forgive me."

"Have you forgiven yourself?" Anna reaches out and clasps my hand.

"I don't think that's a one-time deal." I snap my fingers. "You?"

"Not a one-time deal for me, either. But I'm here in your kitchen, and I'm allowing myself to enjoy it."

"Not just my kitchen, I hope."

Anna laughs, a little flush rising under her freckles.

I squeeze her hand. "How long can you stay? When do you have to get back?"

"I can stay as late as tomorrow morning, but then I absolutely have to go."

"I might have to leave anyway, if they can't get Harry's fever down. You know it will always be like this. Our plans, our time, always getting tossed aside for the kids."

"I know, and my work doesn't fit neatly into nine to five. But we'll manage. We'll work something out." She gives me a little smile, and my heart lifts. Here's some genuine optimism. Anna turns brisk, and stands up for more coffee. She refills her mug, and chatters to me about her plans—something about law school contacts in Muskegon, maybe teaching, seeing one client through a bitter divorce, apparently she also wants to rent Cami's house—and I just have to smile and shake my head in wonder. Here she is in my shirt, no pants, tangled hair standing at attention like a mane around her face, and she's taking command like she was born to it.

She finally takes a breath long enough to notice me grinning at her. "What? What's that face for?"

"There's nothing you can't figure out."

"Easy, tiger. It's not an overnight project. But someday, and I can't promise when..."

"You'll come back to Haven."

"Assuming you'll have me."

"I'll have you anytime." I give her my best crooked grin, the same one I deployed to charm her all those years ago in the school cafeteria, over a Styrofoam tray of square rubbery pizza.

I'd sweep her into my arms and carry her off right now, except the hum of worry about my son won't let me reclaim the abandon of last night, when we left a trail of clothing from the door to the bedroom, then lay entwined and nude as the storm rolled on around us.

She reads my expression as only Anna can. "I'm sure he'll be okay. Kids get fevers all the time." She leaves her coffee mug and comes back to me at the table. She reaches down to run her fingers through my tangled hair.

"Thanks. We'll hope for the best."

Her compassion, her calm, loosens a knot in my chest. I guide her into my lap. We reach for each other, and share a soft, chaste kiss, until my phone rings once more.

"It's Sam."

It seems Harry's fever has already started to come down and he has started to perk up, just on the way to the urgent care clinic. *Murphy's Law,* Sam groans, but they will see the doctor anyway, just to be sure. Sam asks me to hold on, and I can hear her urging Harry to take the phone and talk to me.

Anna stands up and whispers, "I'll be right here when you need me." As Anna walks to my kitchen window and watches the rain lash the windowpane, I know this is finally true.

About the Author

KRISTINA RIGGLE LIVES AND WRITES IN WEST MICHIGAN. Her debut novel, *Real Life & Liars*, was a Target "Breakout" pick and a "Great Lakes, Great Reads" selection by the Great Lakes Independent Booksellers Association. *The Life You've Imagined* was honored by independent booksellers as an IndieNext "Notable" book. *Things We Didn't Say* was named a Midwest Connections pick of the Midwest Booksellers Association. Her latest novels are *Keepsake* and *The Whole Golden World*, which was lauded by Bookreporter.com as "a riveting and thought-provoking page-turner that will appeal to fans of Jodi Picoult and Chris Bohjalian."

Kristina has published short stories in the *Cimarron Review*, *Literary Mama*, *Espresso Fiction*, and elsewhere, and is a former co-editor for fiction at *Literary Mama*. Kristina was a full-time newspaper reporter before turning her attention to creative writing. As well as writing, she enjoys reading, yoga, dabbling in (very) amateur musical theatre, and spending lots of time with her husband, two kids and dog.

For more information about Kristina and her books, visit www.kristinariggle.net.

Made in the USA
Lexington, KY
31 August 2015